Moses Gage Shirley

Shirley's Everyday rhymes

Moses Gage Shirley

Shirley's Everyday rhymes

ISBN/EAN: 9783337265038

Printed in Europe, USA, Canada, Australia, Japan

Cover: Foto ©Andreas Hilbeck / pixelio.de

More available books at **www.hansebooks.com**

Moses Gage Shirley

SHIRLEY'S

EVERYDAY RHYMES

BY

MOSES GAGE SHIRLEY

AUTHOR OF "A BOOK OF POEMS," ETC., ETC.

ILLUSTRATED BY

WILBUR LEIGHTON DUNTLEY

He who wanders widest lifts
No more of beauty's jealous veil
Than he who from his doorway sees
The miracle of flowers and trees
Whittier

MANCHESTER, N. H.:
PRINTED BY THE JOHN B. CLARKE CO.
1892

PROEM.

FOR those who come to nature's shrine,
  And worship all that is divine
In books and places and in men,
  I bring the fruitage of my pen.

For lovers who are blithe and gay,
  For those whom love has never met,
I bring my treasures, hoping they
  May some day fall in Cupid's net.

For those by grief and sorrow tried,
  For those who, single-handed, fight
Against the wrong, whate'er betide,
  And lose their all or gain the right ;

For those who labor, those whom fate
  Has placed in hovel or in hall,
I twine the laurel.   Love or hate
  My verses, now beyond recall.

MOSES GAGE SHIRLEY.

GOFFSTOWN, N. H., April 2, 1892.

CONTENTS.

Shirley's
Everyday Rhymes.

AT LOVE'S DOOR.

AT the door of Love I stood with bated breath,
  A great strong passion flooding all my soul ;
I fancied I could almost cope with death ;
  Should I meet love I never would grow old.

Within my mind were countless visions fair,
  Visions that school girls love to dwell upon ;
I felt the kisses of the balmy air,
  And saw the pearly dewdrops on the lawn.

I thought that life would be an endless dream ;
  I builded castles while I rang the bell.
Ah ! what is life that we must always scheme ?
  Ah ! what is love that we so often tell ?

And as I waited, anxious for a sign,
  The door was opened and I saw a grin
Upon the butler's face as he saw mine.
  I asked for Love, he said Love was n't in.

A SONG OF HOME.

I SING of my home in the valley,
  Under the mountain high,
Where the winds of winter rally,
  And the birds of summer fly.

I sing of the maple olden,
  That grows near the roadside gray,
With many a memory golden,
  Hidden from men away.

I sing of the pleasant landscape,
  The shadowy grove of pines,
That encircles the ancient farmhouse,
  Singing their somber rhymes.

I sing of my kindred living,
  Of my kindred gone before,
Of the dear ones all forgiving
  Who have crossed the threshold o'er.

I sing of my sister in heaven,
  Too gentle to linger here,
Whose memory we have striven
  To keep sweeter year by year.

I sing of the ties that bind me
  To that rural dwelling place,
Of the past I 've left behind me,
  Of the future I must face.

I sing of the thorns and roses,
　Among them all must tread,
And before this brief life closes,
　Our hearts with grief may wed.

I sing of my home in the valley,
　Under the mountain's crest,
Where the winds of winter rally,
　And the birds of summer nest.

WHEN HE WENT TO BOW.

I REMEMBER Uncle Ezra,
　Who departed long ago,
How he used to tell the children
　Of the sights he "see" in Bow.

That was when he was a youngster,
　In his springtime's rosy glow,
When he took his famous journey
　To the neighborhood of Bow.

But he never could get over
　What he "see" and what he "heerd,"
Though the frosts of sixty winters
　Clung about his whitening beard.

And whoever told a story,
　Uncle Ezra was n't slow
To offset it by another
　Some one told him up in Bow.

I have heard the good soul tarried
   But a day and but a night,
Then came back and never ventured
   From old Durham in his life.

Strange he never longed for Boston,
   Or the ocean's ebb and flow.
He was happy and contented,
   Telling what he " see " in Bow.

Many years have circled 'round me,
   Since I used to hear him tell
Of his wondrous trip and stories,
   On them all he loved to dwell.

Still I think there 's many living
   Who believe they 've seen and know
Everything, like Uncle Ezra,
   When they 've been to Bow.

SOCIAL POLITICS.

" I' M for reciprocity," he said,
   And asked her for a kiss.
'T was granted, and his soul was filled
   With Eden's vanished bliss.
"You 're for reciprocity," she smiled
   And nearer to him sat,
" What would you do if you beheld
   A wicked Democrat ?"

SPOONHANCH.

IT'S blowin' out again, I see,
  Up there on the sidehill,
An' in the parster down below ;
  It 's pesky hard to kill.

You may dig it up and burn around
  The roots, but sakes alive !
It beats the deuce how that 'ere stuff
  Is bound to grow and thrive.

When it is cut and seasoned well
  It makes a stiddy fire,
But the man who puts it into wood
  Is worthy of his hire.

It 's crookeder than all get out
  And hard as lignvidy.
Though what I write is gospel truth,
  Some wimen fólks will chide me,

Who rave about its varied charms,
  And call it mountain laurel,
When 'round the farm it 's rated 'bout
  Like yellowweed and sorrel.

But after it gets blowin' out
  I must confess it 's pooty,
Considerin' it 's a pizen bush,
  An' most amazin' rooty.

2

It 's blossoms they air pink and white,
　　Just like the young gals' faces.
A bunch of it will not look bad
　　Stuck in your parlor vases.

You may call it laurel if you like,
　　It won't disturb my rest,
For the old-fashioned name it bears,
　　I 've allus liked the best.

And when the woods are full of birds,
　　And it is time to hoe,
I know when I look on the hills
　　The spoonhanch is in blow.

DEAD AT THE BALL.

[During a society ball in a western city, when the excitement was at its height, a young lady, apparently in the best of health, suddenly reeled and fell among the dancers. At first it was thought she had only fainted, but when her friends hastened to her side, she was dead.]

DEAD at the ball, in youth's triumphant sway,
The flush of health o'erspreading cheeks and brow,
The future gleaming like a golden prow —
Dead at the ball.

Dead at the ball, in all her woman's pride ;
Her starry eyes, her soft, abundant hair ;
Struck down in death amid the young and fair —
Dead at the ball.

Dead at the ball, in life's transcendent spring,
When tides of hope and love and joy ran high ;
How sad to think that one like her must die !
Dead at the ball.

Dead at the ball, her restless feet are still ;
Her eyelids closed, her hands upon her breast,
The record sealed, a mockery, a jest,—
Dead at the ball.

Dead at the ball — the giddy dance of death
We may be dancing in life's banquet hall ;
Fast beats the heart and slower comes the breath ;
Dead at the ball.

THE FAMILY CLOCK.

IT has stood on the shelf this many a year,
   Ticking the time away,
In the humble home where I was born
   In the flowery month of May.
It has stood like a faithful monitor
   Of family joys and cares.
Like the timepiece known in deathless song,
   "The old clock on the stairs."

It has witnessed scenes of joy and mirth
   Around the festive board,
When the deepening shadows fell around,
   And the winds of winter roared.
But under the glow of the evening lamp,
   Warm hearts beat glad and free,
With never a thought of grief to come,
   Under the old roof tree.

It holds more secrets than I can guess,
   Or ever can hope to pen,
As it measures time with its friendly hands,
   Over and over again;
As it ticks away in its sheltered nook,
   With the same untroubled face,
One hasn't the heart to spy around,
   And the vanished past retrace.

What the future may have in store for us
   The family clock may know;

Let us hope for the best as we used to do
　　In our dreams of long ago,
When our friend on the shelf dealt out the hours
　　Of childhood rare and sweet,
And the smiling earth looked beautiful
　　In her bridal robes complete.

It is only a common thing I know,
　　Yet to me it is more dear
Than the famous clock in Strasburg town,
　　That is noted far and near.
Though friends have met and friends have gone
　　From my humble home to-day,
The family clock still holds its own,
　　Ticking the time away.

BETTY SPEAR.

IN a little house she lived,
  Long ago ;
And I 've heard it said
  She never had a foe.

She was always very kind
  Unto all.
And she never robbed poor Peter
  To pay Paul.

I 've heard no beggar ever
  Passed her door,
Hungry, but he thanked her
  O 'er and o 'er.

She was busy at her wheel ;
  How she spun
For the neighbors !   Seems to me
  I hear it hum,

As it did in other days
  That have fled.
Pleasant is the memory still
  Of the dead.

Seems to me I see her now,
  As she stood,
With a kerchief o 'er her head,
  Wise and good ;

Or, with knitting, see her busy
   Sitting there,
As she used to many times,
   In this chair.

Here 's the Bible, old and worn,
   That she used,
Showing oft the holy book
   She perused.

Old-fashioned ?   That is true
   Nowadays ;
Many lessons we can borrow
   From her ways.

And I think among the saints
   Who 've striven here,
We shall sometime meet in heaven
   Betty Spear.

STARS.

WE all are stars, like those above us nights ;
   Some gleam and twinkle with unsteady ray,
  While some shine on with constancy alway,
And others are but passing aërolites.

WILLIAM E. RUSSELL.

ONE of the leaders.   Thou art fortified
    By truth and valor.   Youth and hope are thine
And duty nobly done the countersign.
Where'er thou art, whenever thou art tried,
Thou hast been true to life's divinest aims ;
    Standing for all that men esteem most dear,
    Reproachless and incapable of fear.
When Justice calls thee pleading for her claims,
Thou art a leader worthy of the name,
    As chivalrous as the chivalrous of old,
    Undaunted by defeat, unmoved by gold,
Who sought the heights that conquerors attain.
    Thus I salute thee, reading on thy scroll
The secret of thy knighthood and thy fame.

OUR GROCERYMAN.

EVER heard of Charley Parker, him who keeps the gro-
    cery store
Where you see the shinin' letters PARKER BROTHERS o'er the
    door ?
Well, he 's the nicest fellow that we know for miles around,
And we don't believe his equal in a hurry could be found.

It 's goin' on twelve years or more since we fust with him
    met ;
Then he was postmaster in G ——— , a good one too, you bet,
Jist as perlite and sociable, an' allus tried to please,
No matter if we called for stamps or calico or cheese.

In all our dickerin's with him he has been fair and straight.
He 's allus give good measure and he's allus give good weight,
And we find he 's just the same to-day as what he used to be,
A man with hosts an' hosts of friends an' not an enemy.

One year the people 'lected him to represent the town
Up to the legislatur', and he did the business brown ;
He did n't feel above the folks he used to know afore,
As many are inclined to do who get a chance to soar.

He 's allus been obligin', and used us like a friend,
And we believe he will be the same unto the end ;
An' while we live if news should come to us that he is dead,
We think we would break down and cry, just like a girl
    unwed.

And when we leave this world of care, its sufferin' an' its sin,
We hope sometime that we shall meet our groceryman agin,
And hear the white-winged angels sing up in the courts above,
Where there will be no grief nor pain, but nothin' only love.

LAKE WINNIPESAUKEE.

WELL did the Indians name thee, when of old
    They came across thy bosom's wide expanse,
" The smile of the great spirit."   In a glance
  They saw thy beauty marvelous unroll.
They stood beside thee when the rosy light
  Of morning threw its beams across thy breast,
And saw the day god drive far down the west
  His fiery coursers into clouds at night.
Where once they stood I view the wide expanse
  Of shining water rippling to the shore.
I see the islands and in peace adore
  All of the beauty that my soul enchants,
Where fancy's wings are ever free to soar,
  As o'er the waves the sparkling sunbeams dance.

THE COUNTRY PRAYER-MEETING.

THEY have one at the schoolhouse
 Every Sunday when it 's fair,
And I tell you it 's consolin'
 Jist to spend an hour there.

Where neighbors meet to worship
 Without no style or show,
And no one feels above you,
 There 's where I like to go.

They have a little organ
 That plays the sweetest tunes ;
O, how I love to hear it
 Playin' Sunday afternoons !

An' sometimes when I hear it
 I sit with dreamy eyes,
Fer it kinder hints o' heaven,
 An' the joys of paradise.

I love to hear 'em singin'
 The old hymns an' the new,
It allus seems refreshin'
 And it kinder softens you.

I like to hear the children
 A jinin' with the rest,
Their voices sweet an' tender,
 I think I like the best.

Then there 's the Gospel readin',
  An' the simple, honest prayers,
That exhort us to be godly,
  An keep out o' evil snares.

There we learn about the wisdom
  Of the Father and the Son,
An' how some day we 'll meet them,
  When our work on earth is done.

We learn about the city
  That's paved with shinin' gold,
Where we shall live forever,
  When we get into the fold ;

Where there will be no sorrow,
  No sufferin' or care,
An' if we do our duty
  We will meet together there.

If we do our duty bravely,
  With the angels we shall shout,
When our earthly race is ended,
  And the last prayer-meetin's out.

TO ALLEN EASTMAN CROSS.

[On seeing portrait and reading poetry in Magazine of Poetry.]

A CHAMPION of the good and pure and true,
  I see as I behold your likeness here,
A follower of the art that we revere,
A gatherer of heartsease and of rue,
I read your verses with deep interest through ;
  A poet's soul is speaking in each line,
  Fervid with fancies, reverent, benign,
A sympathy for e'en the homeless Jew,
I find therein a sympathy like dew
  That falls alike on weed and bloom and vine.
Your heart's ideal, may it soar and climb
  To loftier heights, that in the coming time
  You may look out upon a wider view,
Knowing at last what fame indeed is thine.

ORIGINAL HYMN.

[Written for the dedication of the Congregational church in Goffstown, N. H., Feb. 11, 1891.]

WITHIN this holy dwelling
    We meet with glad surprise,
And find a realm of beauty
    Is spread before our eyes.
We hear the organ pealing
    A welcoming refrain,
Hosanna to the Father !
    Accept it in His name.

Accept the window gleaming
    With riches manifold,
The sower and the harvest,
    Blest parable of old ;
Accept the window bearing
    The ensign of a dove,
The Holy Ghost descending
    Upon us from above.

With grateful hearts o'erflowing
    We dedicate to Thee
Our church to-day, O Father.
    Forever may we be
Thy children ; let us worship
    Together till we die,
Then take us to Thy kingdom
    Eternal in the sky.

AS TRUE AS TRUTH.

AS true as truth I would that thou might be,
   Dear lovers whispering of your plighted tryst,
Though unto me love is a dream, a mist,
That overshadows an unsounded sea.

As true as truth I would that thou might be,
   O man, O woman, who would be my friend,
   As true as truth unto the very end,
When nothing lingers but my memory.

JOE ENGLISH.

HISTORIC hill, precipitous and steep
   Beyond the Uncanoonucs' rugged forms,
Ye have, like them, defied the roughest storms
That could be driven with relentless sweep.

Historic hill ! where the brave Indian came,
   Joe English, followed by his dusky foes
   One autumn night.   You know the fate of those
Who fell, and why the summit bears his name.

At last a martyr, the brave warrior's fame
   Will rest secure as does his monument ;
   Unlettered, reaching to the firmament.
Others may fall but his will still remain
Through changing years of glory and of shame,
   Ages and ages after this is spent.

THE DEVIL'S ACCOUNT.

THE devil sat at his desk one day
    Looking his records o'er,
And posting his books in a business way,
    As he often had done before.

" You 'd be surprised," said the evil man,
    " If you knew who dealt with me.
And the business I do inside of a year
    Would astonish you all to see.

" Here is a record I 've just begun
    With a portly millionaire ;
And here is one with a giddy maid
    Who rooms across the square.

" Here is another with Amos Jones,
    On page one hundred and five.
But he 's an old sinner," the devil said,
    " And the meanest man alive.

" In his younger days he ruined two
    Of the nicest girls in town,
And has always tried to uphold himself
    By pulling his neighbor down.

" Here is a record of Polly Smith,"
    And he reached for ledger K,
" Several charges for scandal bred
    In the town of Attelway.

" Here are a number I see are paid,"
   And the devil crossed them out.
" I must send to each of them a receipt,
   For they 're gone on a different route.

" Here are a number of standing debts,
   That in order to get what 's due,
I 'm some afraid," the devil said,
   "That each party I 'll have to sue.

" Here are some mortgages I have held
   Too long," and the devil rose,
And rung up his agents all around,
   And ordered them to foreclose.

DEFEAT — VICTORY.

DO not despair if vanquished in the fight,
   When you have fought the battle valiantly,
Contending for the cause of truth and right.
   Defeat? Ah no! I call it victory.

Cheers rend the air and banners o'er us wave
   When we have conquered and our foes retreat,
But often, when the spoils are gathered in,
   Our victory is bitterest defeat.

3

ELLA WHEELER WILCOX.

SWEET poetess, whose name is on the lips
    Of many thousands, thou whose thrilling words
Have roused them like the songs of waking birds,
When fair Aurora, golden-girdled, trips
Across the land, when clover fields are red
And full of bees, all laden with perfume,
The earth a bride, the time — in June,
When sweetest thoughts and loveliest visions wed,
Sweet poetess, whose songs are blithe or sad,
As varying as a changeful April day,
I pay you tribute, whether grave or gay,
My heart with all a tenderness has shared ;
The while I read them fancy ever links
Poppies and roses and carnation pinks.

THROUGH THE CRAWFORD NOTCH.

WILD, rocky gorges, mountains steep and high,
   On either hand salute my eager sight,
As the swift train goes thundering with delight
Through the great notch whose sentinels defy
The angry whirlwind and the tempest drear.
   Standing like giants, stern, heroic, bold,
   I see those wardens of the hilltops old.

Ere man was born, for many a year
   They held communion from their wind-swept fold ;
Upon those summits, dangerous and sheer,
   The eagles nest ; I see the sunset's gold
Burn on their altars half in love and fear.
   My vision rests while evening draweth near,
And over all the waves of darkness roll.

NOT A LEAP-YEAR GIRL.

MY love for you " he said and sighed,
   " Is like the boundless ocean ;
Whene'er I gaze upon your face
   My heart 's in a commotion."
" Oh, no, it isn 't " she exclaimed,
   " Exactly like the sea,
For there's no tide about it,
   And there isn 't going to be."

TO MY ARTIST.

UPON the steps in manhood's early dawn,
        I hail thee as a brother on thy way
    To the far heights where truth and honor lay
Their costliest jewels.   While the years sweep on
May you ascend above the clouds and mist
        That wrapped the summits often from our view.
    May you press onward, firm of heart and true,
And reach the goal that some, alas ! have missed.
My friend and brother, how can time resist
        Or fortune harbor any spiteful thing
    Against the brave who upward toil and sing
To reach the heights earth's shining ones have kissed ?
    Who keep within their hearts eternal spring
Shall evermore with angels plight their tryst.

THE HIGHEST HEIGHTS.

THE highest heights that human souls may reach
        Are not so far that one should fail and sink
    When half way up.   Take courage, pause and think ;
Though many toilers help direct and teach,
The highest heights that principle attains
        We may ascend if we renew our strength
    Like the bald eagle, until we at length,
From lofty crags, look out upon the plains.

AT MILKING TIME.

AT milking time the lengthening shadows fall
   Athwart the earth ; the slow descending sun
Throws his last kisses unto one and all,
  What hour the sultry summer day is done,
     At milking time.

At milking time we seek the pasture bars,
  And drive the lowing cattle up the lane ;
The cow-bells tinkle, and a few faint stars
  Shine from the sky, the first of evening's train,
     At milking time.

At milking time the cows are driven home,
  And the white liquid fills the brimming pails ;
The milker whistles in a cheery tone,
  While from the woods he hears the answering quails,
     At milking time.

At milking time love's sweetest tale is told
  By happy lovers wandering arm in arm ;
Love, priceless love, that never asks for gold,
  But in the twilight finds a golden charm,
     At milking time.

At milking time the poet's soul is stirred
  With holy thoughts too reverent to pen ;
Leave him in silence if he has no word,
  While darkness falls upon the homes of men,
     At milking time.

WHEN HIS WHISKERS GROW.

OUR little Teddy, he will sit
    Each day and plan and plan
What he will do when his whiskers grow,
    And he gets to be a man.

" I 'll buy me a horse and carriage fine
    As any that 's in the town,
And people will look at me and bow,
    When they see me driving round.

" I 'll build me a house upon the hill,
    In the very latest style,
And marry one of the prettiest girls
    That I know for many a mile.

" I 'll study law for a while, I guess,
    And then for Congress I 'll run,
And if I should ever be president,
    Oh, would n't I make things hum !

" I 'll smoke a cigar and wear a hat
    As tall as Colonel White's,
And into society I will go
    And be one of the shining lights.

" I 'll notice the poor, of course you know
    I should do that now and then,
And try to relieve what suffering
    I could with my tongue and pen."

And thus from day to day he plans
   What he will sometime do.
When he reaches his majority,
   His plans may tumble through.

But I think we are all like Teddy,
   Most of us here below,
Always planning great surprises
   When our whiskers grow.

TO THE PISCATAQUOG.

O BONNY river, I will write
   A poem now for thee,
And like a lover I will sing,
   And you may laugh at me.

As merry school girls often smile,
   And whisper to their friends,
You meet your lovers mile on mile,
   Where 'er your waters bend.

You throw your kisses back to them,
   As on and on you go,
Decked with the morning's diadem
   And sunset's golden glow,

By many a meadow, wood, and farm,
   You hasten on your track,
And dazzle with a dazzling charm,
   Old Mother Merrimack,

As you slide down from breezy hills,
　　Upon your pebbly chute,
Together with the mountain rills,
　　Your children bright and cute,

Where fishermen beguile the trout
　　To leave its cool retreat,
And then go home and lie about
　　Their luck to all they meet.

Piscataquog, an Indian name,
　　The great deer place of old,
Where dusky hunters often came,
　　When evening skies were gold,

And sought in ambush for the deer,
　　Shy-faced they came to drink ;
The barbarous arrow ended fear,
　. Death dyed the river's brink.

But many and many a year has gone
　　Since the birch bark canoe
Came down the stream.　They all have gone,
　　Those men of stout sinew.

No more the deer comes down to drink,
　　When evening turns to gray.
Where forests grew now thrives a town,
　　With lads and lasses gay.

The white man's boat glides o'er the stream
  Where Indian paddles swept,
And love-sought maidens pause to dream,
  Where Indian maidens wept.

O bonny river, onward flow,
  Through sun and rain and fog,
My sweetest fancies ever glide
  Down the Piscataquog.

WHEN WINTER COMES.

THE cheerless monarch of the North
  Unbinds his massive gates of snow,
And from his palace sallies forth
  To bid his silent heralds go

Upon a land that fell asleep
  Amid the grasses brown and sere,
Nor waking as the winds repeat
  Their cadence to the dying year.

Far down the west the shadows flee
  In crimson glory fringed with gold,
To fall in beauty on the sea,
  And all its wonders manifold.

When winter comes our hearts shall feel
  The fires of summer burning warm ;
Beyond this human strife and zeal
  We do not fear the raging storm.

PRIDE.

PRIDE was a poppy growing in the field,
   A blood-red poppy, colored to the heart,
A type of love, the love always a part
Of sensual nature that her votaries shield.

" I boast " the poppy said, " a regal name,
   A kingly crest unvexed by wind or sun."
   But ere the fiery heat of day was done
The stricken poppy bowed its head in shame.

BISHOP BRADLEY.

A POLISHED scholar and a friendly man,
   Whole-souled and pure, his people's joy and
      pride,
   New Hampshire's son, who'st traveled far and wide,
O'er all her hills and to the vatican.
A Bishop, yea, but 'neath his silken dress
   There beats a heart as true, I deem, and kind,
   As any we shall ever know or find
In this old world of sin and sinfulness.
A mind as clean and chaste as Alpine snow,
   Where bloom the flowers of rarest speech and thought.
   His whole existence has been ever fraught'
With noble aims and love to all below.
Ah, what are creeds when we God's chieftains scan ?
   They are as naught when we behold the man.

TO THE GOFFSTOWN POET.

Written by a Woman.

FROM the breezy hills of Goffstown
  Is wafted a zephyr sweet,
Mingled with purest perfume,
  And it falls at the poet's feet.

From those lips it falls like music,
  It rhymes with meter pure,
And it touches the heart of some maiden,
  With the truest love so sure.

Tell me, my friend and poet,
  Bard of the grand old town,
Are your thoughts inspired from heaven,
  Borne down to this world of renown?

What is the name of the angel
  Who gladdens your nights in dreams?
Or walked with you in the pathway
  Beside the silver streams?

Is it love, or delight, or beauty,
  That touches your brow with her hand,
And leaves in the air of old Goffstown
  Music from your heavenly band?

Methinks from some far-away heaven,
  Love beckons from realms afar,
And sends you the key to the portal ;
  They leave not its doors ajar.

TO "A WOMAN."

THESE wimen folks are allus up
   To somethin', I declare ;
It 's just as natur'l for 'em
   As it is to breathe the air.

But I did not suppose that one
   On 'em would think of me,
And write sich flowery lines
   About my style or poetry.

" Are my thoughts inspired from heaven ? "
   To answer ye I 'll try.
Yes, I ruther think that most of 'em
   Were started in the sky.

What is the name of the angel
   That hovers aroun' my bed ?
Goodness, I could n't tell yer,
   So many aroun' me tread.

Is it love, or delight, or beauty,
   That lays a hand on my brow ?
I should think by the pressure on it
   They were all o' em there now.

I 'm much obliged for friendly words,
   An' compliments expressed
About my poems ; wal, perhaps
   A few 'll stand the test.

The question is, Who are ye?
  Somehow I cannot think,
But I 'll wager you 'r as pooty
  As a full blown medder pink.

ROSES RED.

ROSES red, roses red,
    Blossoming in June ;
Roses red, roses red,
    Wafting sweet perfume.

Roses red, roses red,
    Wooed by breeze and bee ;
Roses red, roses red,
    'Neath the apple tree.

Roses red, roses red,
    I will gather you ;
Roses red, roses red,
    For my sweetheart true.

Roses red, roses red,
    Withering away ;
Roses red, roses red,
    Why can you not stay ?

TO J. E. O.

[Formerly pastor Congregational church, Goffstown, N. H.]

THOU standest on the vantage ground of truth,
     Earnest and fearless, battling for the right,
Before the world,— a heaven elected knight,
Thou standest with the quenchless fire of youth
Within thy heart, while old traditions fold
     Their garments round thee, while within thy veins
     Runs the rich blood of Puritanic chains,
Linking thy fate with dauntless men of old.
Thou art endowed with nature's kingly grace,
     Born in the purple, and by justice led,
Looking above thee into heaven's pure space,
     Between the living and between the dead,   .
Seeking aright God's holy word to trace,
     By drawing wisdom fron its fountain head.

AN ALLEGORY.

WHICH shall I choose," a love sought maiden said,
     " Of the two roses that I now command,
One white as snow upon a winter's land,   .
And one like summer's sunsets, burning red.
The first will bring me peace on earth, — above,
     The other, turmoil, tears that fall like rain. "
     She made her choice ; how was it, wise or vain ?
Upon her breast she pinned the rose of love.

OUR FLAG.

Written for flag raising of the village schools, May 30, 1890.

TODAY we lift our banner up,
  Our country's flag and ours,
And dedicate it in the pomp
  Of childhood's happy hours,

We fling our ensign to the breeze
  For which the fathers died,
And as its folds salute the air,
  We feel a conscious pride,

Within our hearts while we recall
  The record it has gained,
The struggles and the trials past,
  The victories obtained,

Beneath its folds where it has swept
  Over the land and sea,
The faithful warder of our homes
  And true democracy.

Baptized on many a battlefield,
  With lead and iron hail,
Yet bravely has it held its own,
  And enemies have failed

To filch from it its honor bright.
  It waves in triumph still,
The ensign of our country great,
  O'er valley, plain, and hill.

To-day we lift it proudly up,
  Our country's flag and ours,
And dedicate it in the glow
  Of springtime sun and flowers.

We lift it up, long may it wave
  Over the schoolhouse here,
Filling each breast with loyalty
  And patriotic cheer !

Long may it wave ! its stars undimmed,
  The stripes still on its folds
When fleeting years have passed away,
  And memory o'er us rolls.

A golden flood of changing scenes,
  This a red-letter day,
We 'll place upon our calendar,
  O schoolmates young and gay.

Let us be worthy of the flag
  This day we dedicate,
And by no evil act of ours
  It's glory desecrate.

When we have laid aside our books,
  And from the school repair,
It will be sweet to know and say
  Our flag is waving there.

MY LOVE, MY OWN.

MY love, my own, when you shall come to me,
    My heart will thrill with love's sweet ecstasy ;
I shall awake and see with clearer eyes
The common things too often men despise.

I shall awake and hear the woodland birds
Singing more sweetly for your cheering words ;
I shall look out on scenes beloved of yore,
Until they widen, widen more and more.

When you draw near, this sameness will grow less ;
When I shall hear the rustle of your dress,
And feel the pressure of your loving hand,
All things will change into a fairy land.

All things will change, but I cannot compare
The old and new, the beautiful and rare,
Until you come, until my eyes shall see
Your own endowed with mutual sympathy.

My love, my own, when shall I see your face ?
When shall I meet you ? in what trysting place ?
Or must I sing, or must I weep alone ?
Shall I not find you, O my love, my own ?

4

WHO IS WHO AND WHICH IS WHICH.

SUM people think it 's cunnin' to run their nabors down,
  And git up all sorts o' stories about the folks in town,
But when the thing is changed around I notis it don't hitch,
For it makes a heap o' difference who is who and which is
    which.

Sum people like to dicker with other folks' affairs,
And amon' your sweetest posies they most allus look fer tares.
If you don't know where ter place 'em, they will run you in
    a ditch
Sum day and then inform you who is who and which is which.

Sum people like ter tread upon another feller's toes,
And tew pass a poor opinion now and then about his clothes ;
But when the feller gits aroun' his thoughts with theirs don't
    mix,
And so he gits instructed who is who and which is which.

When woman slanders woman, and uses lots o' chin,
Perhaps it goes fer nothing an' you don't reckon it a sin ;
But wait until the proper time, fer all sich things will keech,
And you will soon disciver who is who and which is which.

It makes a heap o' difference, as I remarked afore,
But when you get to heaven, where Saint Peter tends the
    door,
Somehow I have a notion that amon' the poor and rich,
It 'll not count much in glory who is who and which is which.

RECOGNITION.

"HOW sweet the hour when we at last obtain
 The recognition we have sought for years,
 Often alone with eyes suffused with tears ;
As we toiled upward from the lowly plain,
Seeing above us cold and barren 'heights,
 Whereon the vultures brooded for their prey,
 Fainting and heart-sick, struggling day by day,
' Till Fortune claimed us as her favored knights.
How sweet to know that we at last have gained
 The recognition that is truly ours !
 To bow our thanks o'er jeweled hands and flowers,
And friendly offerings upon us rained.
 How sweet the hour, but O how sad to state,
 That recognition often comes too late !

BRAKES.

"PLEASE may I have some of those ferns ? "
 A city maiden said
One day to honest Farmer Burns,
 " Oh ! what a lovely bed."

The farmer smiled and bowed his head,
 " Take all you want, land sakes !
You call 'em ferns, a lovely bed,
 But all I see is brakes."

LINES

Written on receiving some flowers from a young lady in the South.

HOW kind of you to send these flowers
　　I hold within my hand,
Gleaned from your garden's rosy bowers,
　　In your own sunny land.

Where mocking-birds sing all the day,
　　And sweet magnolias blow,
While I look out upon a land
　　Made desolate with snow.

My garden flowers died when winds
　　Of autumn shook the trees.
Hushed is the cheerful song of birds,
　　The drowsy hum of bees.

But in this fragrant gift you send
　　The summer's brightness burns,
And all its beauty and delight
　　For me again returns.

I hear the robin in the lane
　　Call blithely to his mate,
I see the lengthening shadows fall,
　　The cattle at the gate.

And over all the sunset's gold
　　Burns brightly overhead,
Till sinking down into the west,
　　It fades when day has fled.

I thank you for the little gift
  Gleaned from your garden bowers,
A bit of southland that has cheered
  A few dull wintry hours.

I wish you joy, I wish you health.
  May love, true love, be thine,
And blossom sweetly as the flowers
  Down in your sunny clime.

ON THE DEATH OF A YOUNG MAN.

TAKEN from all the scenes he loved,
    From all that he held dear,
In the first flush of manhood's pride,
  When heaven and earth drew near.

Taken, when just before him lay
  His future bright and fair,
When Fortune beckoned him to climb
  And all the world to dare.

Taken when love and hope beat high
  Within his manly breast ;
Called from the turmoil and the strife,
  To find eternal rest.

Taken from home and kindred dear,
  And every loving tie ;
He is not dead, he liveth yet ;
  The good can never die.

Why do we weep? the Father knows
 And cares for every one
That he calls home. Sweet be the rest
 Of this beloved son.

Peace to his ashes evermore !
 Who heeds the Father's call
Can have no fear, for heaven and home
 And life are given all.

Who come and lay their armor down,
 Bright with the glow of youth,
And bear upon their silent lips
 The deathless seal of truth.

Are they not heroes? Yea, I hold
 It is not years that tell,
So much as duty nobly done,
 Who fights life's battle well.

Sleep, loved one, sleep, the fray is past,
 Your battles here are o'er.
The world has lost but heaven has gained
 One valiant spirit more.

A NEW IDEA.

"OH, papa, " said little Nellie,
 And a bright thought to her springs,
" What ailed the fallen angels,
 Could n't they work their wings ? "

TO A BUMBLEBEE.

AH, Mr. Bumblebee, I'm glad
    To see you sporting here
Upon my window. You're the first
  That I have seen this year.

Your pantaloons are black as jet,
   Your waistcoat's striped with yellow,
And taken all around I find
   You quite a jolly fellow.

I like to hear you bumping 'round
   In the good-natured way
You always do when trees leave out
   And flowers bloom in May.

I like to see you waltzing here
   Upon this window pane,
And pity you when you get left
   Outside amid the rain.

Miss Hollyhock, it's whispered low,
   Calls you a gay deceiver,
And if you don't dispel the doubt,
   Of course I must believe her.

She claims last summer you appeared,—
   What makes you look so silly? —
And courted her awhile, and then
   You wed Miss Tiger Lily.

But after all, you 've only done
    What many swells of fashion
Are doing every day, neglect
    And kill the tender passion.

You may be right.   Supposing I
    Had dwelt in pleasure's bowers
I might have kissed as many pretty girls
    As you 've kissed pretty flowers.

WHEN I AM GONE.

WHEN I am gone, I ask you not to cry ;
    If you have loved me, rather smile and say,
My friend he is at rest somewhere to-day.
        When I am gone.

When I am gone, O lay me 'neath the flowers
    That I have worshiped with an artist's eye,
    And with a poet's soul that love supply.
        When I am gone.

When I am gone, some message may remain,
    Some words of hope, some memory to cheer,
    That will grow sweeter with each fleeting year,
        When I am gone.

YOUR SOUL.

IT'S a wonderful thiug, ever boundless and deep,
   That mystery freighted 'mong surges that roll,
From the depths of infinity endless its sweep, —
            Your soul.

It 's a valuable thing, and too dear to be sold
   For the fruitage of sin, which is darkness and mold,
That treasure within, up or downward its goal, —
            Your soul.

THE BRAVEST OF THE BRAVE.

YOU may sing of the mighty ones of earth,
   Who have lived and passed away ;
Of the ancient kings who once held forth
   With the most despotic sway.

You may sing of the brave who to battle go,
   And die on the battlefield,
With their faces turned to the sullen foe,
   Their fates by the conflict sealed.

You may sing of your heroes, alive or dead,
   Of the names that fame has blessed,
But the man who conquers his foes with love
   Is braver than all the rest.

MAIDEN'S LOVE SONG.

O DEAREST love ! why dost thou wait
 So long outside my garden gate ?
The roses blossom red and white,
And song birds carol day and night.

O love, why dost thou linger yet ?
The autumn woods are damp and wet,
The birds have flown, the bees have fled,
My garden roses all are dead.

O love ! thou art a laggard still.
The snowflakes glisten on the hill,
My heart with hope sings sweet and low
The songs it sang thee long ago.

Where'er thou art, anear or far,
O come and be my guiding star,
The star of life, my destiny !
O come, dear love ! and bide with me.

MONUMENTS.

THE finest monuments that men erect
 Have little value whereso'er they rise,
Unless they tell of some good action wrought,
 Some noble work that time cannot disguise.

LINES TO A PORTRAIT.

[Suggested to the author on seeing his portrait hanging in a printing-office under a
knot of white ribbon, tied by a young lady compositor.]

BESIDE a window, near a printer's case,
    I found my portrait hanging up one day,
Under a ribbon tied with jaunty grace
    By dainty fingers laboring for pay.

In the dim office, where the jar
    And crashing tumult of the busy press,
Our finest thoughts can either shape or mar,
    The silent tribute flattered me no less

Than had I found it in a parlor wide,
    Hanging with other portraits on the wall,
Near works of art that touch a poet's pride,
    And fill his mind with wonder or appall.

What does it mean ? Who runs can read, I know,
    The message that the simple act demands
From her who tied the ribbon's dainty bow,
    And fastened it in place with girlish hands.

It means that I must keep my record pure
    And free from sin and every evil strife,
Or fame's sweet flowers I cannot procure,
    The symbol of a good and virtuous life.

So let it be.   May she who left it keep
    Her soul as pure as the exalted trust
That God demands ; for what we sow we reap,
    After our hearts are buried in the dust.

AN APPLE TREE IN BLOSSOM.

WHAT can be fairer, may I ask, than this,
    An apple tree in blossom, pink and white,
Whose blossoms are sweet children of delight,
That love the zephyrs' and the sunbeams' kiss?

What can be fairer, may I ask, than this,
  An apple tree in blossom, white and pink ?
  An apple tree in blossom, let me think ;
I cannot say, unless some dainty Miss.

What can be fairer, may I ask, than this,
  An apple tree in blossom in the spring,
  The choice of lovers and all those who sing
The sweetest songs of nature's bridal bliss.

THEY ARE STRANGERS NOW.

MISS Gushingway writes to her beau,
    " Dear Charles, I have been ill,
And to prolong my life, I think
  The doctor taxed his skill ;
He said of nothing I must think,
  And he might pull me through ;
But, dearest, all the while I lay
  And thought and thought of you.''

DOWN AT AMOSKEAG.

WHAT pleasant memories hover 'round,
    Of happy days gone by,
When down at Amoskeag we strayed,
  My humble muse and I !

Sometimes we were alone, again
   Some friendly spirit walked
With us along the dusty way
   And cheered us as they talked.

Again I see the grocery store,
    And all the friends held dear
Come trooping 'round me as I write,
   And fill my heart with cheer.

I see the schoolhouse near the road,
    The children at their play,
Whose cheerful shouts and merry looks
   Come back like birds in May.

Once more I stand upon the bridge,
    And looking down below,
I see the swirling waters foam,
   As oceanward they flow.

Here at the falls, in days gone by,
    An Indian chieftain's daughter,
Seeking her lover, met her fate
   In the mad foaming water.

You 've heard the story, without doubt,
   Of this romantic nook.
Get Whittier's poems, turn and read
   " The Bridal of Penacook,"

And you will understand it all ;
   Who reads the sad affair
Will feel a thrill of pity
   For the maid who perished there.

I see Rock Rimmon's titan form,
   Breasting the sunset line,
Beyond the Uncanoonucs lift
   Their peaks in storm and shine.

Across the river on the east,
   Kissed by the morning sun,
Rests the old hero, General Stark,
   Who fought at Bennington ;

While the Queen City of the state
   I see is near at hand,
With all its thriving industries,
   And riches to command.

On scenes like these I love to dwell,
   However small or big,
But I must close.   Long life to all
   My friends at Amoskeag.

MORNING MIST.

I CAN see it on the meadow,
  And along the sloping hill,
And over on the river,
  In the morning calm and still,
Until the sun has risen,
  And his bride, the earth, has kissed,
And the bridal veil is riven,
  The veil of morning mist.

TALMAGE.

THOU great divine, whose eloquence has stirred
  The hearts of thousands, listening to thee,
Thy fame has spread to lands beyond the sea.
The name we write is now a household word.
Thy thoughts we trace upon the printed page,
  And find a solace reverent and deep,
  A prophet's voice, a mighty grasp and sweep,
No other has in this conflicting age,
Isaiah like, if I may liken thee.
  Thou hast no peer in realms of piety.
With holy thoughts that searching minds engage,
  Thou stand'st alone, original, intense,
Seeking the right, all evil to assuage,
  As one assured of heavenly recompense.

UNCLE BEN TO THE MINISTER.

WELL, parson, seein' we have met,
    An' I have heerd you preach,
I 'm thinkin' that a rhyme or two
    Would do no harm to each.

I hope you 'll overlook the fact
    That I 've not been to college,
An' make allowances for what
    I lack in art and knowledge.

I 've wrote of men an' trees an' brooks,
    An' folks say I 'm a poet,
Altho', perhaps, by my address
    A stranger would n't know it.

About your preachin'? Well, I find
    It allus sets me thinkin',
Though sum prefer a different kind,
    That gits the eyes to winkin'.

I find that you adhere to facts
    An' reason more than fancy,
But then, perhaps, I cannot see
    The same as Jane an' Nancy.

I 've heard most of 'em preachers talk,
    Down in the neighborin' city,
But none of 'em, I think, are more
    Engagin' or more witty.

5

It may be I 'm behind the times,
　　An' sort o' absent minded,
Altho' I think unto the truth
　　My eyes were never blinded.

I 'm thinkin' if our Lord should come
　　Among us as of yore,
That there are folks who would to-day
　　Abuse him as before.

Some folks alive git no deserts,
　　Fer evil actions done,
But they will have to square accounts
　　When this 'ere life is run.

They say some people go to church
　　Jest to display their clothes,
An' care no more about the Word
　　Than I for punkin blows.

It may be they 're a leetle like
　　The Pharisees of old,
Who thought they knowed more than the rest,
　　Whose wisdom was pure gold.

But like the guilty king, who saw
　　The writin' on the wall,
Sich folks are weighed, an' soon or late,
　　False pride will have a fall.

Sum folks pertend to sympathize,
   An' use the finest speech,
Which may be all correct an' well,
   If they *do* what they preach.

For I believe whene'er we try
   To reach the bottom facts,
That true religion is n't words
   So much as it is acts.

JAMES WHITCOMB RILEY.

HE is the dearest minstrel of our times,
   Whose quaint sweet numbers reach the pub-
     lic heart,
From time to time, in country and in mart.
Who has not read and treasured up his rhymes,
So full of pathos, eloquent and deep,
   Whose humor sparkles like a mountain rill ;
   Droll and peculiar, leading at his will
Our fancies,— now we laugh and now we weep,
As he leads on.   How his creations fill
   My mind as I recall what I have read !
   Before me is a sumptuous banquet spread ;
I see " Jap Miller " down at Martinsville ;
   The sweetest fragrance all around is shed,
   For the " old-fashioned roses " blossom still.

LITTLE SISTER.

LITTLE sister, thou art sleeping
In that home beyond the grave,
Where the angels watch are keeping
Over all the true and brave,
Far removed from sin and sorrow,
In this human world of clay,
Where our striving wants may borrow
From its gifts that fade away.

But in that eternal Aiden,
Spotless lilies form a crown
For each pilgrim, heavy laden,
And the aching heart crushed down ;
Where the immortelles cluster
Fadeless, not like those of ours,
Which through years will lose their luster,
Like all common earthly flowers.

Would that I could paint your beauty,
Gentle dreamer, in thy home,
Roused no more at call of duty
And where sickness never comes ;
Only as a child face beaming
With the joy of children's love,
Happy with a sense of gleaning
Treasures from that court above.

Not forgotten here, but living
    With her Saviour and with God,
Freed from all the unforgiving
    Spirits of a servile sod ;
Yes, sometime I 'll know thee better,
    Little sister, when the King
Shall unbind each prisoned fetter,
    And I hear the loud harps ring.

THE MOOSEWOOD IS IN BLOW.

I LOVE to look upon the land
    After the winter's snow
Has vanished from us.   Once again
    The moosewood is in blow.

I love to hear the robin sing,
    The brook with joy o'erflow,
And smell the perfume in the air ;
    The moosewood is in blow.

I love to see the crimson buds
    Upon our maples glow,
Kissed by the morning's rosy beams ;
    The moosewood is in blow.

I love to wander o'er the hills,
    Where winds are soft and low,
When 'mong the alders in the swamp
    The moosewood is in blow.

Again I hear the blackbird call
  Unto his friend, the crow,
My friends,— I find them everywhere ;
  The moosewood is in blow.

When all the land is full of song
  Our hearts no grief should know,
No bitter tears should fill our eyes ;
  The moosewood is in blow.

LINES

Written on a visit to the Yacum Springs House, Goffstown Center, N. H., August 4, 1890.

THE summer day was drawing to a close.
    We left the train and hastened to the spring,
  A dusty traveler, noting everything.
The while the sunset deepened into rose,
And died away, in a luxurious doze ;
    The landscape lay, a half-unconscious thing,
    Begemmed with dew, a picture for a king.
While evening came,— a picture of repose
We found around us, save the big hotel,
    Aglow with light and youthful beauty rare,
    Exchanging greetings, passing here and there,
Till all grew silent as the moonlit dell,
    Then slumber stole o'er duty's guarded lines,
    Soft as the wind among the neighboring pines.

THE WOMAN OF THE PAST.

THE woman of the past has gone forever from our view,
    And is numbered with the mighty host, the valiant and
        the true,
Who have passed beyond the portals to that home of rest
    sublime,
Up whose shining steps eternal the white winged angels climb.

The woman of the past was tried, but in the darkest hour
Her womanhood rose glorified, and blossomed like a flower,
Amid the changing scenes of war, and avarice, and hate,
A worthy record she has left, undimmed by time or fate.

The woman of the past stood firm for liberty and truth ;
No honest labor she despised,— industrious as Ruth,
She stands amid the harvest field on history's golden page ;
We seek but cannot find her type in this prosaic age.

The woman of the past was good, and virtuous, and fair,
And with a lavish hand she strewed rich blessings everywhere.
No devotee of fashion, but in simple modest dress,
She came and she departed, with a smile to cheer and bless.

The woman of the past was kind, and sought by word and
    deed
To make the whole world better.   O, how I love to read
Her story, as 'tis handed down from records quaint and old !
Forever let it be enshrined, and evermore be told.

The woman of the past has gone forevermore, alack !
Unnumbered years now intervene, we cannot call her back ;
Upon the woman of to-day our longing eyes are cast,
But we can never hope to find the woman of the past.

THE WOMAN OF THE PRESENT.

THE woman of the present is a sweet, alluring thing,
And quite as sentimental as the songs to-day we sing.
She is fond of beaux and dancing, and enjoys a merry time,
And her followers declare that she's a creature most divine.

The woman of the present is a paragon of style,
But the fellow who can win her love deserves her sweetest
   smile.
She's a girl whose fads and fancies often take us by surprise,
Though at heart she may be honest, and conservative, and
   wise.

The woman of the present has a thousand charming ways,
And despite of fashion's hobbies is a subject meet for praise ;
Despite the imperfections that are common to us here,
If she does her duty nobly, she 'll be noted in her sphere.

The woman of the present loves to mingle in a crowd,
But the choicest specimens you meet are neither vain nor
   proud.
You 'll find her in the tennis court, and often book in hand,
And when you walk or drive with her, you 're in enchanted
   land.

The woman of the present is inclined to flirt, it 's said ;
We 'll let that question go, and ask if she can make good
    bread,
And further ask if she can make good cake and apple pie,
That would one's appetite appease and cause them not to die.

The woman of the present, as we leave her to her fate,
We hope some day she 'll win the love of a congenial mate ;
And what we cannot understand or fully comprehend,
We trust she 'll overlook and still consider us her friend.

THE WOMAN OF THE FUTURE.

O THE woman of the future ! I can see her through a
    haze ;
She is coming minus bustle, she is coming minus stays ;
I can see her through the shadows of the present's misty light,
She is coming, she is coming, like an angel of delight !

The woman of the future ! O, how beautiful she seems,
As in fancy I behold her in the brightest of my dreams ;
In fancy I behold her, and I long to hear her voice
Ringing down the pleasant valleys, " I am coming, O rejoice!"

The woman of the future will not trifle with our hearts,
She will find more time to study into sciences and arts ;
She will not be too disdainful, irreverent, and proud,
But with all the highest virtues and attainments be endowed.

The woman of the future will be modest in her looks.
She will sing the sweetest ballads and peruse the choicest
    books ;
Her sympathies will widen, and her goodness will extend,
Until the poor shall bless her, and the weak shall call her
    friend.

The woman of the future will not throw herself away,
For the ballroom's giddy pleasure, bringing wrinkies and
    decay ;
Nor drink the honeyed nectar of enchantment, long and deep,
Sowing seeds of dissipation that in anguish she must reap.

The woman of the future will come to us as pure
As the fragrant Easter lilies, and her fame will rest secure ;
When she comes to dwell among us, in her eyes that light
    will be
That we have never seen upon the land nor on the sea.

O, the woman of the future will be generous and brave,
And her honor she will cherish without blemish to the grave.
In joy I wait her coming, she will blossom like a rose,
And her heart will find a lover who is worthy to propose.

A GROVE OF PINES.

HOW shall I draw them with a poet's pen ?
How shall I paint them with an artist's brush ?
Those sturdy pines that grow within the glen,
Where, wandering, I have heard the sweet voiced thrush ?

If I could paint them in their living green,
Ah, what a picture they would truly make !
If I could draw aright each forest scene,
The very limbs would bend and rock and shake.

If I should paint them when the wind was loud,
There would be war and knights in armor dressed ;
You would behold the branches interlace and crowd,
You would behold each warrior's battle crest.

If I should paint them when the wayward wind
Grew calm, there would be happiness and love ;
Nothing but lovers who have never sinned,
Nothing but bright and sunny skies above.

How shall I paint them, when along the west
The sun goes down in one bright sea of red ?
When every song bird seeks its sheltered nest,
And I look out, and lo ! the day is dead.

THE EVENING TRAIN.

WITH a rattle and roar I can hear it come
    Over the track a mile away,
As from the station I see the sun
    Sink down in the west at the close of day.

There are shy-faced Amy and Rose and Bess —
    Three of the nicest girls I know —
Who await its coming with eager eyes,
    As they pace the platform to and fro.

There is Deacon Brown, with his snowy locks,
    And Farmer Jones and dear Aunt Kate,—
God bless them all, though I often smile
    When I hear them ask if the train is late.

And here are the boys with their roguish ways,
    Ted and Jimmie and Frank and Paul,
Gathered in groups with their little mates,—
    May the heavenly Father keep them all.

There blows the whistle ! I hear the bell,
    And look for the headlight's lurid glare,
As the iron monster swiftly comes,
    Bearing its treasures of love and care.

It has slackened speed, it has stopped, and now
    Its precious burden of souls alight ;
The car man signals, again it goes
    With a rattle and roar into the night.

Awhile there are greetings and friendly looks,
　　As the waiting throng salute each friend ;
Then the station closes, and, one and all,
　　The people go to their journey's end.

When the battle is fought, and no more we feel
　　The daily struggles of want and gain,
May we get our tickets and sing in glee,
　　As we leave for home on life's evening train.

AT SCHOOL.

I OFTEN think we are but scholars here,
　　Striving together to obtain success ;
The respite from our duties, great or small,
　　May be a nooning or a brief recess.

Experience is the teacher, stern yet kind ;
　　The world we dwell in is the common school,
And if we strive to learn our lessons well
　　In it we only need the golden rule.

And when at last from out the world we go,
　　Meeting together at the heavenly gate,
It may be well for us if we upbear
　　The record of a worthy graduate.

AT SET OF SUN.

AT set of sun the daylight quivering dies;
　　Along the west the shadows, fold on fold,
Drop their dark curtains o'er the sunset skies
　　As gently as a lover's tale is told,
　　　　At set of sun.

At set of sun, amid the murmuring pines,
　　The crescent moon her silver brooch displays;
Amid the branches full of somber rhymes,
　　She keeps her tryst, while falls the purple haze
　　　　At set of sun.

. At set of sun the silence grows more deep,
　　Deeper for study, meditation, thought,
　Hallowed by vigils the rapt soul must keep
　　Sweeter by loving all that love has brought,
　　　　At set of sun.

At set of sun our wearied limbs may rest,
　　After the heat and turmoil of the day ;
And hearts find solace, weary minds oppressed
　　Grow calm until the sorrow dies away,
　　　　At set of sun.

At set of sun, when all the sky is red
　　With crimson blushes, we may be called to go
Into the night to meet our loved and dead
　　In that fair land where heavenly breezes blow,
　　　　At set of sun.

BETTER.

BETTER to smile while we live than frown,
　Better to love than to gain renown.

Better to comfort some aching heart
Than to do in battle a warrior's part.

Better some narrow path to tread
Than a highway ending in shame and dread.

6

BESSIE.

I KNOW of none that 's neater,
  More fair to look upon ;
She cannot read our meter,
  Or laugh our words to scorn.

She does not care for candy,
  Or caramels, or gum ;
She loves no fickle dandy,
  Nor flirts with any one.

She never drank the beverage
  Of the soda water fount ;
Her rank is near the average,
  If you will take account.

She never goes to dances,
  She never plays croquet ;
Her mind don't run to fancies
  That will carry her away.

She has no hammock swinging,
  In any shady nook ;
Nor has a voice for singing
  No more than has a rook.

There is a look pathetic
  Within her dreamy eyes,
Though she 's not so æsthetic
  As some might wish, or wise.

She does not care for dresses,
　　As you must soon allow ;
Who is she then ?　Who guesses?
　　Why Bessie is a cow.

WORSHIPERS.

THE miser worships at his treasure chest,
　　And counts his gold with crafty eye and zest,
He little cares who prays and goes to church,
If for new treasures he can only search.

The lover worships at a different shrine,
Until the worship seems to him divine,
Hallowed with beauty he cannot express,
One word may gladden and one word distress.

The maiden worships at the shrine of truth
With innocence, the innocence of youth,
A modest look within her eyes down cast,
A reverence only truest reverence hast.

The poet worships earth and sea and sky,
And finds expression in the wind's deep sigh.
A friend of nature, near his heart is hers.
What do you worship ?　All are worshipers.

AGAIN IN SPRING.

A GAIN in spring the maples are a-bloom
    With crimson tassels.   All the forest trees
Feel the new change and murmur low like bees
      Again in spring.

Again in spring the sweet arbutus shows
Its starry flowers, wooed by rain and sun ;
In wooded dells they open one by one,
    Again in spring.

Again in spring the purple violets bloom
Upon the hillsides, where the balmy air
Comes like a solace after grief and prayer,
    Again in spring.

Again in spring the birds with joy return
From southern lands, their music to repeat ;
From marshy bogs the frogs arise and peep
    Again in spring.

Again in spring love's sweetest tale is told ;
The old, old story has an added charm
To youthful lovers wandering arm in arm,
    Again in spring.

Again in spring the poet draweth near
To nature's heart ; he feels the pulses leap
Within his own,— deep calleth unto deep,
    Again in spring.

Again in spring the tender grass upshoots
Its emerald spears up through the parent sod ;
Who worships nature must be near to God,
    Again in spring.

Again in spring, sad heart, forget thy cares,
And feel that love encircles everything ;
That up to glory lead life's winding stairs,
    Again in spring.

A CITY BOARDER.

A H, she's a girl that's dashy,
   And she's a girl that's sly.
She's decked in colors flashy,
   To catch a fellow's eye.

She flits across the meadow,
   And she flits across the lawn.
She makes a gaudy spread, O,
   She laughs our words to scorn.

She seeks among the clover
   For the four-leaf clover spray,
For she's a merry rover,
   And rambles all the day.

She talks about the city
   With all its varied charms,
But thinks it is a pity
   To leave the pleasant farms.

She's "gone" on novel reading,
   And on poetry she's intense,
And only shows her breeding
   In a lack of common sense.

Her cheeks are like blush roses,
   She's nimble as a roe,
And sweeter than the posies
   That all around her blow.

Her eyes are full of magic,
  And play with cupid's darts,
Until the play seems tragic
  For many youthful hearts.

Ah, she 's a little daisy,
  And dearly loves to flirt,
She 's enough to make you crazy,
  She is so trim and pert.

Where'er I see her going
  I gently heave a sigh,
For I think she 's just as knowing
  As a summer butterfly.

THE WORLD MOVES ON.

AH, what is man and a man's emprise
    Of love and laughter and scorn !
To-day he lives but to-morrow he dies,
  While the world keeps moving on.

O lovely woman, whose charms we sing !
  Your beauty will pass away
Like a tale that is told, like a sweeping wing,
  And clay will soon mix with clay.

Our heroes we name may live for an hour,
  While the poet wins lasting fame ;
In the years to come his thoughts will flower,
  Though the world goes on the same.

WHITE CLOVER.

NOT as thy sister blooms dost thou appear,
   Showing a queenly form and purple crest.
Amid the grasses thou in white art dressed,
Emblem of virtue, true democracy,
Sought by the pilgrim butterfly and bee,
Who find a solace on thy dewy breast,
Kissed by the zephyrs, wafting thy perfume,
Sweeter to me than that from southern lands,
Where dark-eyed lovers follow love's demands,
And all the air is drunk with sensual bloom.

I hail thee coming when our earth is fair,
Amid the vernal beauty of the year,
Full of sweet sights and sounds to eye and ear,—
The songs of warblers and the sunset sky
Bring back to memory pleasant days gone by,
When life was new and beauty everywhere.
The laurels are abloom on vale and hill,
Wild roses and sweet-briars blossom still,
And for their beauty I have given praise;
But the white clover blooming here and there
Amid the grasses seems to me as fair.

TO DEATH.

WHEN thou shalt come to seal our fleeting breath,
   When all our labors here on earth are o'er,
Deal kindly as with others gone before,
And fold us gently in thy arms, O death.

REPENTANCE.

"I HAD a dream," he said, "the other night,
  That my lost love came back to me again,
  Regretting that she ever gave me pain.
Her cheeks aglow, her eyes all dewy bright,
She came and offered me her jeweled hands ;
  They trembled and I felt the old delight
  Arouse my heart and flood my weary brain,
Forever dreaming of the infinite."
She said, " Forgive me if I have done wrong ;
  My love was frail, but yours, O yours was deep ;
  Too deep to fathom — I can only weep,
And pray to heaven that I might atone,
  But if I cannot, as you think it meet,
  May death's dark mantle over me be thrown."

BEFORE SHE THOUGHT.

"YOU 'RE the first girl I ever kissed,"
  He said with beaming eyes,
And drew the maiden to his breast,
  Thinking he 'd won a prize ;
But when she spoke it seemed as if
  He 'd have to faint away.
" O, Charlie, that is just what all
  The other fellows say ! "

HE IS MY FRIEND.

HE is my friend who finds in everything
    Something to praise ; who casts beneath his
        feet
All false ideals, yea, who scorns deceit.
        He is my friend.

He is my friend who loves the good and true
And hateth evil with a holy ire,   .
Who nerves himself to conquer and aspire.
        He is my friend.

He is my friend who throweth narrow creeds
Unto the wind, and like the wind is free,
Whose mind is broad, who loves humanity.
        He is my friend.

He is my friend who scorns to lead astray
The pure in heart from the highroad of right,
Who ever guards them like a gallant knight.
        He is my friend.

He is my friend who tries, though he may fail,
To reach the goal that he afar has sought,
Who moves mankind by earnest deed and thought.
        He is my friend.

He is my friend who offers me his hand,
And never shrinks to welcome me with cheer,
Whene'er we meet, a peasant or a peer.
        He is my friend.

He is my friend who hastens to my side,
And like a brother would my name defend ;
Though others fail me yet will he abide.
       He is my friend.

BAD COMPANY.

A GOOD man once, who had a likely son,
    Was pained to see him seeking evil ways,
For bad associates had led him on ;
    The father thought that sin might end his days.

And so one day he called him to his side,
    Holding some shining silver to the light,
Fresh from the mint he showed it to his son,
    Together with some coppers not so bright,

And said, "Observe me, I will put the coins
    Within my pocket.; let a few days pass,
Then ask to see them and I will explain
    Why I have called you ; now you need not ask."

The son was some astonished, but he went,
    And left his father sitting in his chair ;
He could not think why he had called him in,
    And mused upon it in the open air.

Some days went by before the son bethought
    That he would ask his father what it meant,
But in due time he came to him and learned
    Why at the first for him the father sent.

" Observe," the good man said, " this silver now,"
   And drew it forth to meet his eager sight.
His eyes fell on it, it was black and charred,
   And did not sparkle when it met the light.

" Association did it ; as the cents
   Have changed this silver once so bright and new,
So will the bad associates that you keep
   Have very much the same effect on you."

We can append a moral if you like,
   But being useless we forbear to speak,
For it is very evident and clear,
   That folks will judge us by the crowd we seek.

ONE OF THE BOYS.

I LIKE that phrase that soldiers often use
   When they recall their sorrows and their joys,
For every hero with them, great or small,
   Is " one of the boys."

Far rather would I win a soldier's fame
   Than seek for wealth when avarice destroys,
Then, when I 'm gone, beside my grave you 'd say,
   " Here lies ' one of the boys.' "

LONG, LONG AGO.

HOW sweet to dream of pleasures that have fled,
Of sunny hours that, full of joy, we led,
Long, long ago.

There is a charm that words cannot define
About the past, its story and its rhyme,
Long, long ago.

Something we ponder o'er from day to day,
But ever dim it seems and far away,
Long, long ago.

Who does not dream of pleasures that have gone,
Of sunny hours when sweetest hopes were born,
Long, long ago?

I SAW HER FACE.

I SAW her face as it was turned aside
From one who loved her with his heart and soul,
She smiled in scorn; his love was never told,
I saw her face.

I saw her face again in after years,
When it was scarred by suffering and tears,
The roses gone, of youth no lingering trace,
I saw her face.

SURRENDER.

SURRENDER unto truth and honor high
   Establish in the halcyon days of youth ;
Be brave and generous as the years go by ;
      Surrender unto truth.

Surrender unto love ; let base desire
   Lay down its arms, and, like the gentle dove,
Gain an affection that will never tire ;
      Surrender unto love.

Surrender unto God, ye sinning soul,
   And seek the path where shining feet have trod ;
Look upward, where the stars in glory roll ;
      Surrender unto God.

THE LEAVES ARE FALLING DOWN.

OCTOBER comes among the trees,
   October's woods are brown,
There is a comfort in the breeze,
   The leaves are falling down.

Within the woods, the forest grand,
   And the maples in the town,
Seem painted by an elfin hand,
   The leaves are falling down.

Upon the hills the goldenrod
  Has doffed its yellow crown,
Its seeds are scattered on the sod,
  The leaves are falling down.

The squirrels seek their winter's store,
  And hide it in the ground,
The farmer beats his threshing floor,
  The leaves are falling down.

Give us the peace, give us the rest,
  So quiet and profound,
When autumn is with glory dressed,
  The leaves are falling down.

A QUESTION.

IN the eyes of the world she was a hateful thing,
  An outcast woman, full of grief and shame,
With many errors traced against her name,
Which once was fair, in youth's transcendent spring.

Hated by those who bowed her to the sod,
They go unscathed while she remains their prey.
Which will fare better when they 've passed away,
And each shall look into the eyes of God ?

TAKE YOUR CHOICE.

FIRST there comes the vernal poet,
　　In the spring to have his say,
When the lilacs are in blossom,
　And the organgrinders play.

Next, the ice-cream poet rhymeth,
　In the balmy month of June,
Of the mixture and his sweetheart,
　When the roses are in bloom.

Then the autumn poet sigheth,
　O'er the glories that have fled ;
Like a love-sick girl he murmurs,
　And will not be comforted.

After him the snowflake poet,
　To ye editor repairs,
And from out the little office
　Springs in anguish down the stairs.

THE CRIMSON STAIN.

SIN leaves a stain, like that upon the key
　Old Bluebeard's wife strove vainly to wash out.
While looking in the face of destiny,
　We should be careful what we are about.

A GOOD NAME.

Cattle die, kinsmen die, one's self dies, too, but the fame never dies of him who has won a good name.— NORSE SAGA.

BETTER than gold or silver,
　Better than jewels rare,
Better than kingly coronets,
　Is the record we should bear.

Better than great possessions,
　In houses and in lands,
Is the worthy title we should own,
　With full or empty hands.

Better than transient glory,
　Better than things that fade,
Richer than treasures olden
　To lover and to maid.

Cattle die and kinsmen
　Pass on, the saga reads,
While everything is fleeting,
　Change after change succeeds.

One thing remains immortal,
　The world cannot disguise;
Amid the change unchanging,
　A good name never dies.

7

FOR YOU AND ME.

FOR you and me the sunsets burn;
　　For you and me the birds return,
The flowers bloom, the ships sail by
Like fleecy clouds across the sky.

For you and me the mountains hold
Their stores of silver and of gold.
The brooklet gushes sweet and clear
For you and me the changing year.

For you and me the balmy air,
And beauty reaching everywhere;
The fairest rose that summer brings,
The sweetest song the robin sings,

The ripest fruit of autumn store,
The cricket chirping by the door,
The winter evenings cold and still,
The snowflakes on the window sill,

The wisdom found in school and books,
The outstretched hand, the pleasant looks
Of those we meet from day to day,—
Our friends upon the dusty way.

For you and me this gift of life,
The calm repose, the battle's strife,
The days gone by, the days to dawn,
For you and me the night and morn.

For you and me a dream of fate,
A heart to love, a heart to hate,
Some fields to reap, some fields to sow,
Ere life is ended here below.

For you and me the hours glide,
The ocean bringing in its tide,
The things we know and hear and see,
Behold ! they are for you and me.

For you and me one God to love ;
For. you and me one sky above,
Forever old, forever new ;
For you and me the stars shine through.

For you and me such things are for ;
For you and me a natural law,
The stormy wind, the ocean wave ;
For you and me a grass-grown grave.

For you and me some tears to shed,
Some straight and narrow paths to tread,
A round of sorrow and of mirth ;
For you and me six feet of earth.

For you and me some loss and gain,
Some joy to share, some secret pain,
Until each life shall cease to be,
For death will come for you and me.

For you and me a home afar ;
For you and me a shining star ;
For you and me the angels wait ;
For you and me the pearly gate.

For you and me a soul within,
A soul to guard from strife and sin,
Until our warfare here shall cease ;
For you and me a time of peace.

For you and me beyond the sun
Unfading laurels to be won ;
Beyond the shimmering jasper sea,
A home of rest for you and me.

RELEASED.

THE door was opened and the warbler flew
  Out of the cage into the heaven's deep blue,

Singing a song of gladness in his flight,
As on he sped through leagues of glimmering light.

Out of its cell one day a human soul
Into the realm of endless beauty stole,

And like the bird, from prison bars set free,
Soared upward into heavenly ecstasy.

OVER THE LINE.

OVER the line we will some day pass,
    You and I.
Into that wonderland vague and vast,
    By and by.

Over the line we will softly tread,
    Wrapped in a spell,
To those beautiful gardens beyond the dead,
    Of the asphodel.

Over the line with the radiant throng,
    When will it be ?
The time may be short or it may be long,
    For you and me.

Over the line, but it matters not,
    If we are prepared,
And the battle of life have bravely fought,
    And its triumphs shared

With all who suffer and moan and toss,
    O heart of mine !
Tenderly, bravely, let us cross
    Over the line.

ELOPED — TELESCOPED.

HE loved her, fondly, but too well,
    And since she has eloped,
The people stare at him and say,
    " His heart is telescoped."

WE'RE DRAWING NEAR.

WE 'RE drawing near unto the portals blest,
The sunset glories gleaming in the west,
Where, free from sin, our spirits shall abide
In endless bliss upon the other side.

We 're drawing near to life's mysterious close,
The land of rest, the haven of repose,
Where, free from grief, no more on earth we 'll roam ;
We 're drawing near to our eternal home.

THE HEART'S IDEAL.

THE heart's ideal should be throned on high,
Above the petty ills that fret us here,—
Should be uplifted to a wider sphere
Of aspiration, nearer to the sky.

Though pleasant landscapes all about us lie,
And the great ocean marches o'er its dead,
Be not deceived, for shining overhead
Are greater wonders than we have passed by.

The heart's ideal, upward is the cry,
Above the petty ills that fret and cheat
The glory of our lives, above defeat,
And sordid motives that with passions vie
To drag us down, until we find retreat
Impossible, and, full of anguish, die.

YOUR SWEETHEART.

I 'M your sweetheart, don't you love me?
　See ! the skies are blue above me,
All my soul with joy is ringing,
Tender fancies to you winging.

I 'm your sweetheart ; red with blushes
Are my cheeks, while madly rushes
Through my veins life's crimson glory ;
Whisper low, the old, old story.

I 'm your sweetheart, take me to you ; .
Though the fiends of hate pursue you,
Love like mine no fate can sever,
I 'm your sweetheart now,-- forever.

THY WAY IS BEST.

THY way is best ; the glitter and the sheen
　Of other paths beside it are but dross,
But shifting sand beside it and the cross.
　　Thy way is best.

Thy way is best ; the conflict and the pain
Will soon be o'er and we shall be at rest.
Help us to say when life is near its close,
　　Thy way is best.

I LOVE THE WOODS.

I LOVE the woods, each sylvan nook and bower
   Wherein the wild bird chants its roundelay,
And frisky squirrels chatter all the day ;
      I love the woods.

I love the woods, I know them every tree,
Each sturdy oak, each song enchanted pine,
The maple and the birch are friends of mine ;
      I love the woods.

I love the woods, the deep sequestered woods,
Where silence broods and solitude is known ;
There like a Dryad let me build my throne ;
      I love the woods.

I love the woods, the spirit haunted woods,
Where echoing footsteps often seem to tread,
A wonderland, where fairies meet and wed ;
      I love the woods.

I love the woods, the purling brooks that run
Leaping and laughing like a guileless boy
O'er roots and stones, exuberant with joy ;
      I love the woods.

I love the woods ; have I not been with them
When fair Aurora kissed away the night,
Or when the stars shone through them clear and bright ?
      I love the woods.

I love the woods in sunshine and in storm,
When summer zephyrs gently move their boughs,
And the rude wind of winter through them soughs ;
      I love the woods.

I love the woods ; morning and noon and night
Have I beheld them now for many a year.
As I grow older they become more dear.
      I love the woods.

I love the woods, though Amphion come no more
To charm them as he did when once of old
He made them rise and dance to music bold ;
      I love the woods.

I love the woods ; O lumbermen, beware !
Do not despoil them needlessly for gain.
Riches have wings and avarice has pain.
      I love the woods.

I love the woods, yea, as a lover loves
The idol of his heart.   On moonlit eves
I love to wander 'neath the rustling leaves ;
      I love the woods.

I love the woods, where the shy partridge drums
And the pink mayflowers blossom in the spring,
Sweet haunt of rest, of which the poets sing ;
      I love the woods.

I love the woods.   When lengthening shadows fall
Around me and I pass beyond your ken,
One thing I crave that you will say to men,
      He loved the woods.

WHO BRAVES DEFEAT.

WHO braves defeat and struggles bravely on
From day to day amid the world's disdain,
I count a hero worthy of the name,
Who braves defeat.

Who braves defeat and battles for the right,
To truth and virtue consecrates his soul,
He is a hero heroes should extol,
Who braves defeat.

Who braves defeat when everything is lost
That he held dear, when all is swept away,
He best can prove who love him or betray,
Who braves defeat.

Who braves defeat, I offer him my hand.
Kind fortune guide him through the dust and heat,
He yet may conquer, he may yet command,
Who braves defeat.

A KNOWNOTHING.

"I DON'T know anything," she said,
Her eyes on me were set.
She was the wisest, fairest Knownothing
That I have ever met.

GOLDSMITH.

DEAR, gentle Goldsmith! When I read his life,
　　Full of perplexities and troubles rife,
There always is compassion in my heart,
A love for him, a reverence for his art.
No truer poet ever lived than he,
None ever voiced a sweeter minstrelsy
Than his, as sweet as was the flute he played
Among the peasants, and a wanderer strayed.
He is a wanderer still, but up above,
Where there is peace and recompense and love,
More ample than he found while here below,
A pilgrim in a land of grief and woe;
His verses live, and to the world have gone,
Sweet as the hawthorn blooms beneath the thorn.

RECLAIMED.

WHERE once there was a waste of desert sand,
　　Now fertile gardens gladden all the land.

Where the fierce simoon o'er the desert blew,
Now falls at even heaven's refreshing dew.

Within a soul held long in error's snare,
Dwells a free spirit sanctified by prayer.

Poor desert land! Poor soul by error chained!
Once ye were lost but now ye are reclaimed.

WHEN LOVE IS TOLD.

WHEN love is told, we wonder if the spell,
  Of glad surprise will thrill us through and
   through,
Making old objects seem again like new,
  When love is told.

When love is told and crimson blushes dye
Our loved one's cheeks, will tears unbidden come?
Will she be speechless, full of passion, dumb,
  When love is told?

When love is told will sweeter flowers bloom
Beneath our feet where thorns grew wild before?
Shall we admire beauty more and more,
  When love is told?

When love is told will bitter longings die?
And every evil that assails us now
Be put away and friendly thoughts allow,
  When love is told?

When love is told will heart respond to heart,
Fighting life's battles, fearing no defeat
From winter's chilling winds or summer's heat,
  When love is told?

When love is told shall we look down the west,
And see the sunset fringed with richer gold,
Feeling a holy calm of peace and rest,
  When love is told?

AFAR.

AFAR, I reverence all the good and true,
   Whose pilgrim feet have sought the shining
      heights,
Through days of sorrow and through starless nights,
For whose great gifts the world must ever sue.

Afar, I worship all that is divine ;
   Is there not glory on that far-off sea ?
   A land of promise veiled in mystery
Beyond it and the dim horizon's line.

Afar, I love ; O love, wilt thou draw near,
   And bring sweet solace into heart and brain,
   Forgetting sorrow and forgetting pain ?
By loving love all things will be made clear.

MAJORY JASPER.

MAJORY JASPER, she 's the girl I love with all my heart,
   And who I hope some day to wed, and say to grief
      depart ;
Her cheeks are like the damask rose that blooms beside my
   door,
Whose falling petals in the wind are tumbled o'er and o'er.

Her eyes are like the summer sky, kissed by the shimmering
    sea,
When all the land is full of song, and youth and love agree ;
Her lips are like the cherries red that in my garden grow,
And her bosom it reminds me of the winter's drifted snow.

Her step is nimble as the fawn's, that o'er the mountain speeds,
Her life is pure and beautiful and full of quiet deeds,
And that is Majory Jasper ; she has given me her heart,
And I — some day — I wed her, and say to grief depart.

Though enemies assail me and troubles bow me down,
I 'll bear affliction bravely and never wear a frown ;
Though all the world should hate me and its venom at me
    cast,
I 'll care not, for Majory says she 'll love me to the last.

THE BOYS.

THEY'RE jolly good fellows, every one,
    Frank and Arthur and Fred,
And all of the other lads I know,
    Active and go-ahead.

They 're always ready to cheer us on,
    As we meet them day by day,
With a friendly word and shake of the hand,
    Along life's dusty way.

Reckless you call them, my doubting friend?
  Reckless?   Is that the truth?
Nay, high resolve and desire yearn
  To-day in their splendid youth,

To reach the heights where the great have trod,
  On the pinnacles of fame,
To love and to win the love of men,
  And die with an honored name.

In the years to come my prayer will be,
  That their hearts may still be young,
Men that the knell of endless youth
  The years have never rung.

Men with the happy spirit still,
  They kept in their boyhood days,
Ever aglow with the chivalry
  That is seeking and merits praise.

Still marching on in the battle's din,
  In the noontide heat and glare,
Imbued with a holy confidence,
  Willing to do and dare.

Thus may they go through sun and shade,
  Fighting as heroes fight,
Upon their standards no sinful stain,
  Their helmets agleam with light.

After the spurs and laurel won,
    May they find the sweet repose
That comes to all who have bravely fought,
    When the battle is at its close.

Men may pass by me and women deceive,
    And empty may seem life's joys.
My barque may be tossed over stormy seas,
    But I 'll never forget the boys.

AT THE LANGMAID MONUMENT.

UPON this spot her mangled form was found.
    Poor Josie Langmaid, what a death she died,
While on her way to school, and evil eyed
The spoiler came and felled her to the ground,
A maiden pure and blameless as a child !
    O cruel hands, to seek her youthful life,
    Half bud and blossom, with a murderous knife,
And leave her dead within this forest wild !
    Her blood was shed, a crimson sacrifice
    To sin and passion ; thou hast paid the price
All murderers pay who slay the undefiled.
    A tragic tale for one to hear or write,
Though her freed spirit sings in paradise,
    While his is groping in Plutonian night.

8

STABBED.

O IT wasn't any sword thrust that caused his heart to
    bleed,
This champion of the beautiful in word and thought and deed
It wasn't any dagger that pierced him through and through,
No work of steel that made the wound he guarded from our
    view.

O it wasn't any sword point, or javelin, or spear,
That sought the breast and wounded our gallant young com-
    peer ;
For it was a meaner weapon, and I warn you, old and young,
To never stab another with a hateful, jeering tongue.

HE PAYS THE PRICE.

HE pays the price who seeks to climb above
    His fellow-men and jeer the crowd below,
For honor's bubble and for glory's glow ;
        He pays the price.

He pays the price who barters love for gold,
    Who slays affection in his happiest days,
    Winning the world's approval or its praise,
        He pays the price.

He pays the price who follows passion's sway,
    And gives himself a living sacrifice,
    To sin and death, and darkness and decay,
        He pays the price.

STRANDED.

POOR Crusoe, stranded on his lonely isle,
  With eager eyes oft sought the distant sea,
Waiting for some propitious breeze to blow
  Unto his home a friendly argosy.

Day after day he watched, until at last
  His prayers were answered by a favoring gale,
And, full of gratitude and joy, he cried,
  "A sail! A sail!"

Poor human souls are stranded, even now,
  On lonely isles of sin and doubt and woe,
And many have been praying now for years
  For favoring winds a ship to them to blow.

When it shall come, O joy too deep for words!
  May they behold it, may they live to hail
Their longed-for harbinger of peace and joy,—
  "A sail! A sail!"

OPPORTUNITY.

I AM the goddess of delight and fame;
  I bring good gifts to cheer the heart and eye;
But you will not receive me, and at last
  Bemoan your fate when I have passed you by.

THE GIRL I DIDN'T KISS.

I OVERLOOKED her in a crowd
  Of lads and lasses gay,
The prettiest little girl, I deem,
  That ever came my way.

'T was at a party years ago,
  Over in number three,
Where we had many pleasant games
  And jovial company.

I did not mind her 'round the rope,
  Perhaps she was so small,
And there were lots of bigger girls,
  More elegant and tall.

I overlooked her 'till the last,
  This little blossom sweet,
And as I was about to leave,
  Somehow our eyes did meet.

A tender smile spread o'er her face,
  Rare as the afterglow
Of sunset, pure and beautiful,
  Such as the angels know.

I see her now as she was then,
  A young and happy child,
Her hair was like the raven's wing,
  When she upon me smiled.

Again I see that upturned face,
  But I was vain and proud,
And left her with a careless look
  Amid the passing crowd.

Again I see that little basque
  And overskirt of red ;
Maybe the wearer is alive,
  And maybe she is dead.

I often wonder at her fate,
  Amid the world's cold din,
Whether she kept her record bright,
  Or tarnished it by sin.

'T was years ago, but yet to-night
  My heart with grief is filled ;
I might have kissed her, but I know
  'T was as the angels willed.

'T is ever thus, I find, in life.
  Our dreams of earthly bliss
Are saddened by the memory
  Of the girl we did n't kiss.

RICHES.

THAT man is rich, though he may never own
  A single acre on earth's boundless breast,
Who finds new wonders in each shrub and stone,
  And golden glories gleaming in the west.

RECOMPENSE.

SOMETIME, I think that all who labor here
   Will be rewarded at some future time
  For useful work ; it may be yours and mine
That will find praise where men now scoff and jeer.

Sometime, I think that justice will be just
   To rich and poor, to publican and saint,
   On her escutcheon there will be no taint,
And on her armor there will be no rust.

Sometime, I think the citadel of sin
   Will be bombarded by the hosts of right ;
   Its minions have assailed, with hate and spite,
But at the last the hosts of right will win.

Sometime, I think the time will soon be meet,
   For those oppressed by error and by wrong,
   To seek redress with valiant hearts and strong,
And rule victorious after sore defeat.

Sometime, I think that evil thoughts will die
   That have wrought death to many loved ones here,
   And slander's baleful tongue will lisp in fear
After its victims give to it the lie.

Sometime, I think that virtue will arise
   Victorious o'er the carping fields of doubt,
   Her foes within, the jealous foes without,
Will be brought low and shame will fill their eyes.

Sometime, I think that love will claim its own
   In the dim future we cannot forecast ;
   Our longing hearts will feel its thrill at last,
Though we have hungered, hungered and alone.

Sometime, I think that when we all go hence,
   And leave the world that will not aid us now,
   Although in sorrow we still wait and bow,
Sometime, somewhere, there must be recompense.

WHAT HAVE YOU DONE ?

WHAT have you done to overpower sin,
   That walks abroad and gathers in its grasp
The whitest souls, to poison like an asp?
     What have you done ?

What have you done that you may dwell in peace
And feel no winds of passion o'er you blow,
No bitter blasts of penury or woe?
     What have you done ?

What have you done that you may have no fear
When death shall come and say to you, " My friend,
Your work is o'er, now seek with me the end ? "
     What have you done ?

YALLER WEED.

SUM people think it 's pooty
    An' call it goldenrod,
But I find it 's tarnal rooty
    When it gets inter the sod.

It 's growin' in the parstur,
    An' it 's growin' on the hill,
Where'er you cum across it
    It 's pesky hard to kill.

I find it when I 'm mowin',
    Fer it 's gitting in the grass,
An' afore I am a knowin'
    Will be in my garden sass.

It like ter spilt the honey
    One year when I kept bees.
Perhaps you think I 'm fooling,
    Just taste it if you please.

An' if you don't find it bitter,
    Much bitterer than gall,
You may tee-he and titter,
    And laff at me, that 's all.

If them ere summer boarders
    Pertend to love it so,
I think it is a pity
    It cannot with them go.

Them folks who make up poems
   May praise it to the skies,
Because they know no better,
   An' see with different eyes.

But we farmers are agin it,
   It is so bad to seed,
An' find no virtues in it,
   This common yaller weed.

FORGIVE ME.

FORGIVE me, Lord, I pray,
   For what I 've done amiss,
For what I 've left undone,
   While now the rod I kiss.

Forgive me for the sins
   Committed in thy sight.
Though scarlet they appear,
   Yet thou canst make them white.

Forgive me ! I am frail,
   And only common dust ;
Though enemies assail
   Forever thou art just.

Forgive me, Lord, I pray,
   O may I be forgiven !
And with a childlike faith
   Draw near to Thee and heaven.

LOVE.

LOVE answers love, I think, sometime, somewhere ;
    It may be here, it may be over there,
Where angels sing, in heavenly courts above,
Sometime, somewhere, I think love answers love.

OCEAN SHELLS.

TOYS of the ocean's surging waves,
    Dashed in the clefts of rocky caves,

Left on the mountain top or lea,
Swept in the past by an unknown sea,

Found with the driftwood washed ashore,
Tossed where the angry billows roar,

Out of the tempest's spiteful reach,
Lashed by the tide on a sandy beach,

Pressed to the seaweed damp and limp,
Kissed by some sporting water nymph.

In that mystic age when the Gods of Love
Pictured their deeds in the stars above,

Sought for their heroes amid the shade
Of the purple twilight undismayed,

And held communion amid the deep,
Where its heaving waters together sweep.

Shall we be with them when life is spent,
And the somber ferryman is sent

To bear our souls to the other side?
Shall we see them all through shadows wide?

Oh Charon ! spare us this mortal dread
We have of the harbor of the dead.

Echo a song from thy inmost cells !
Sing of the sirens, ocean shells !

THE VILLAGE POSTOFFICE.

IT' S nigh unto four miles away,
　　But then I like to go
Once in a while and get my mail,
　　Down there at the P. O.

The buildin' is a stylish one,
　　An' the office that 's inside
Is about as neat and pooty
　　As any I have eyed.

It 's finished up in hickery
　　Of that ere blackish kind,
Perhaps you 'd call it walnut,
　　But then it doesn't mind.

The boxes air as trim and sleek
   As any I have seen,
And everythin' is orderly
   About the hull machine.

He uses every one alike,
   Our courteous P. M.,
Whether they love the G. O. P.,
   Or style themselves a Dem.

Sometimes I have to wait until
   The mail is sorted 'round,
And then I see the loveliness
   And beauty of the town.

I mean the gals and ladies now —
   God bless 'em every one —
With all their curls an' furbelows
   An' dresses factory spun.

Jest see them school gals waitin'
   With smiles an' nods an' winks,
My stars ! they 're most as pooty
   As a bunch o' medder pinks.

Or a lot o' garden posies,
   A hull bed of 'em in blow,
I don't know what 's the sweetest,
   They all delight me so.

The flowers I might gather
   Into a big bokay,
An' the gals,— I 've tried to gather 'em
   Into my rhymes to-day.

An' now I hope they 'll all keep fresh,
    And the good book peruse ;
An' if they ever think of beaux
    The very best will choose.

An' as I take my mail an' leave
    Light hearted, there are some
Who go in grief. God pity those
    Whose letters never come.

MASKERS.

This world is a grand masquerade and we are all maskers.—Milton.

WE are maskers all in this world to-day,
    On the stage of life our parts we play.

Maskers all ?   Is it not the truth,
We begin to mask in our very youth ?

Old and young, both great and small,
To-day are holding high carnival.

For the sake of the world we must bow and smile,
Though the heart may be breaking all the while.

And thus we go through sun and shade,
Till death shall close our masquerade,

And the play shall end and the curtain fall,
And the masks be taken from us all.

KEEP YOUR POT A-BILIN'.

A HOMELY sayin', I admit,
  Yet full of golden fillin',
The adage that they spake of old,
  Of " Keep your pot a-bilin'."

And yet to-day it seems as good,
  And full of pithy meanin',
As when 'twas spoken years ago,
  A sword of logic gleamin'.

Friend, are you laggin' in a rut ?
  Your rusty wheels need 'ilin' ;
If you would keep up with the crowd,
  Your pot must be a-bilin'.

If obstacles are in your way,
  And evil thoughts beguilin',
Now is the time to thin 'em out,
  And get your pot to bilin'.

Now is the time to look ahead,
  Before you 're one day older,
You may get landed in a ditch,
  Or run agin some bowlder.

Do what is right and what is just,
  And after you get started,
You 'll find the olden adage good,—
  Here 's to the tender hearted.

If you would win success and fame,
   And git the big world smilin',
And huggin' you with all its might,
   Just keep your pot a-bilin'.

— ...

UNCLE WILLIAM.

UNCLE WILLIAM, he 's been dead
   Forty years or more,
But the record that he left
   Oft I ponder o'er.

Everybody knew him well,
   In and out of G ——,
And they said no better man
   Ever lived than he.

All the children used to say,
   " Uncle William 's good."
And his word was held as law
   In his neighborhood.

Seems to me I see him now,
   As he used to go,
Driving o'er the country roads,
   Moderate and slow.

Nothing mean about the man,
   Honest to a cent,
Courteous to rich and poor,
   Said just what he meant.

Loved his neighbor as himself,
  Spread no evil news,
Always cheerful at his work,
  Spurned the trickster's shoes.

Always willing to relieve
  Suffering and distress,
Never passed the needy by,
  Or the fatherless.

Hypocrites and shams aroused
  All his holy ire;
If there was a hell, he thought
  They would feel its fire.

He was always good and kind
  Unto man and beast,
Deeming that the great in heaven
  Here are rated least.

Over forty years have gone
  Since he went away,
But I wish that there were more
  Men like him to-day.

MODESTY.

I LIKE that native modesty which bears
  Its honors meekly with each round of praise;
  That does not yield to passion's lurid blaze,
A primrose growing in a field of tares.

THE TIME WILL COME.

THE time will come when we must say farewell
    To all we love, to friends both far and near.
    The smiling landscape, everything held dear,
Will pass away in one transcendent spell.

The time will come when love for love will plead,
    And hearts unmoved will feel a sweet desire,
    A holy passion sweeping into fire,
Till loved and lovers have been blessed indeed.

The time will come when jeweled hands will twine
    The laurel wreath around the poet's name,
    Who wrote of love and virtue without fame,
And, dying, all his words became sublime.

The time will come when justice will disdain
    To please the few, but to the many give
    Her goodly favors, if the many live
So as to merit all they rightly claim.

The time will come when death, the common foe,
    Will level all in high or low estate ;
    The humble peasant and the potentate
Will fare alike in one impartial show.

The time will come when we shall be forgot,
    And buried 'neath the daisies out of sight,
    Unmindful of the world's regard or slight,
Its mighty battles false or bravely fought.

9

ONLY A LITTLE WHILE.

ONLY a little while to read
    Of the wonderful days gone by,
To worship our heroes, in thought and deed,
  Under the azure sky.
      Only a little while.

Only a little while to sing
  The songs that are truly good,
To feel the quickening thoughts they bring
  To us for our spirit's food.
      Only a little while.

Only a little while to fight
  For the needy and oppressed,
To battle wrong with the sword of right,
  In the name of holiness.
      Only a little while.

Only a little while to walk
  In the worldly path of sin,
Where the demons of hate defile and mock
  The stricken soul within.
      Only a little while.

Only a little while to go
  From that darkness into light,
To turn aside from its grief and woe,
  To struggle and win the fight.
      Only a little while.

Only a little while to gaze
  On the ocean's heaving breast,
To comfort those who need our praise
  And our love before they rest.
      Only a little while.

Only a little while to cull
  The flowerets sweet and rare,
To know that our earth is beautiful,
  And nature is ever fair.
      Only a little while.

Only a little while to long
  For those heights beyond our reach,
For the shining tablelands of song,
  Too eloquent for speech.
      Only a little while.

Only a little while to hold
  The hands that are warm and kind,
To learn that friendship can soon unfold
  New beauties to heart and mind.
      Only a little while.

Only a little while to love,
  As all loving hearts must do,
The holy things below, above,
  In God's own retinue.
      Only a little while.

Only a little while to seek
  For life's mysteries unveiled,
With wrinkled brow and faded cheek,
  And eyes by want assailed.
    Only a little while.

Only a little while to live,
  Only a little while
To pardon foes and their ills forgive,
  Though we weep as we try to smile.
    Only a little while.

Only a little while to dream
  Of that marvelous city afar,
Whose golden turrets glimmer and gleam
  To us like the morning star.
    Only a little while.

Only a little while to wait
  Till the angel death shall come,
And silence alike the poor and great,
  And beauty's lips be dumb.
    Only a little while.

POETRY.

THOU art the language of the wind that blows,
  The light that glimmers on the distant sea.
The poet finds thee prisoned in a rose,
  But everywhere thou art, O poetry !

TRABBLIN' ON TO GLORY.

WE are trabblin' on to glory,
 We are trabblin' day by day
To de eberlastin' city,
 Up beyon' de milky way.

CHORUS — We are trabblin' on to glory,
  We are trabblin' on.

We are trabblin' on to glory,
 An' ole Satan he's behin',
But he'll git lef' mos' awful,
 W'en no sinnahs he can fin'.

CHO.—We are trabblin' on to glory,
  We are trabblin' on.

We are trabblin' on to glory,
 Now, chillun, take yo' stan',
An' you'll hab no trouble
 To fin' de promise' lan'.

CHO.— We are trabblin' on to glory,
  We are trabblin' on.

We are trabblin' on to glory,
 O sinnah, come erlong !
Come an' learn de gospel story,
 In de halleluyah throng.

CHO.— We are trabblin' on to glory,
  We are trabblin' on.

UNTO THE END.

UNTO the end I hold that we should keep
　　The love we win, the virtues we profess,
Unto the end, whate'er we sow or reap,
　　The voice of duty will demand no less.

Unto the end I hold that we should love
　　All noble things, all aspirations deep,
The earth below, the arching sky above,
　　Whether we live in joy, or doubt, or grief.

Unto the end I hold that we should hate
　　All evil things, all things that overthrow
The mind's surcease, and open not the gate
　　For love to enter, bringing peace below.

Unto the end I hold that we should dwell
　　With holy thoughts ; the poorest may aspire,
May train his soul within its narrow cell,
　　To follow truth and conquer base desire.

Unto the end I hold that we should sing
　　The sweetest songs and praise the purest art,
With a pure reverence, pure for everything
　　That draws us nearer unto nature's heart.

Unto the end I hold that we should pray
　　For larger faith to see and understand ;
What seemeth night may widen into day,
　　And narrow vistas into worlds expand.

Unto the end still seek the loved and lost,
  Who have been with us,— now we call them dead,
Struck down in youth by death's untimely frost ;
  Believe them living and be comforted.

Unto the end be good and brave and true ;
  Have courage, O my brother and my friend !
There is so much, there are so few to do,
  Let us be faithful, faithful to the end.

SHE IS NOT HERE.

SHE is not here ; in vain I seek her face,
  Smiling upon me as it did of yore ;
I wait her coming, but she comes no more ;
      She is not here.

She is not here ; no more shall I behold
The love-light shining in her peaceful eyes,
Serene and beautiful as evening skies ;
      She is not here.

She is not here ; no more her gentle hands
Shall seek my own, and love's electric thrill
Arouse my being. Everything is still ;
      She is not here.

She is not here, for God has called her home,
Out of this world with all its sorrows drear,
Into his presence, nevermore to roam ;
      She is not here.

TO HIM WHO WAITS.

TO him who waits amid the world's applause,
　　His share of justice, toiling day by day,
All things will come now dim and far away,
　　　　To him who waits.

To him who waits, beyond the darkness drear,
The morning cometh with refulgent light,
Bringing assurance of a day more bright
　　　　To him who waits.

To him who waits, though tears may often fall,
And knees be bowed in sorrow and in prayer,
All grief will end and everything be fair
　　　　To him who waits.

To him who waits and reaches out his hands
To aid a toiler up life's beetling crags,
Surcease will come from every ill that flags
　　　　To him who waits.

To him who waits, and struggles not in vain
To overcome the evils that abound
Within his breast, sweet will the victory sound.
　　　　To him who waits.

To him who waits there comes a wily throng,
Who sneer and scoff and look with baleful eyes ;
But what of them ?　They are but gnats and flies
　　　　To him who waits.

To him who waits there must be recompense
For useful work, whatever may betide,
A compensation reaching far and wide,
      To him who waits.

To him who waits the stars are always friends,
The restless ocean and the azure sky ;
All things in nature speak and prophesy
      To him who waits.

To him who waits true love will some day come,
And lay an offering at his blameless shrine ;
Life will be love and love will be divine
      To him who waits.

To him who waits the world will some day cheer
And sing his praises ; Fame's mysterious gates
Will open for him ; heaven seem more near
      To him who waits.

THE PURE IN HEART.

THE pure in heart, are they not sanctified
   By God's pure love and holiness within ?
  Aye, sanctified against the ways of sin
And evil things for which men oft have died.

Are they not pure in spirit as the wind
  That sweeps the hilltops when the day is fair ?
  As pure in spirit as the heaven sent air,
The pure in heart, for they have never sinned.

The pure in heart, O they must stand alone,
  And often battle to secure the right ;
  Aye, single handed they must wage the fight,
Until no evil motive has a home.

Within the hearts of those by sorrow tried,
  Chained with the chains of passion and despair,
  Help them to conquer every foe through prayer,
Until the bitter tears of grief are dried.

The pure in heart are all God's children true,
  And if they love him they will see his face,
  Shining in glory from his dwelling place,
When he shall call them at the last review.

Aye, they will meet him and will not depart
  From that fair city fashioned not with hands.
  Some day they will behold the heavenly lands,
And dwell with him for aye, the pure in heart.

LIFE IS TOO SHORT.

LIFE is too short for any vain endeavor,
    For useless sighing over vanished days ;
No time for scorn, no time for needless praise,
    Life is too short.

Life is too short for envy to be nourished,
For sin to cumber up the path we tread ;
Think of the suffering, hear the cry for bread !
    Life is too short.

Life is too short for avarice to devour
And rob men's souls to seek its evil end,
No time for bitter thought, you know, my friend,
   Life is too short.

Life is too short to waste in tears and grieving
Over the love that came but did not stay ;
'Tis sweet to dream, but dreams, too, pass away ;
   Life is too short.

Life is too short ; forgive and be forgiven,
While yet we linger ; everything is brief,
There is no time for idleness or grief ;
   Life is too short.

NOW OR NEVER.

NOW or never, you must do
  Deeds of valor, passing through
Storms and sunshine, day by day,
Safe upon the heav'nward way.

Now or never you must fight
To uphold the truth and right ;
Unto justice give your hand,
Loving home and native land.

Now or never you must bring
Balm for heart's that's suffering,
And a deeper feeling share
With all minds oppressed with care.

Now or never you must climb
Upward to the peaks sublime,
Leaving trivial things below,
Upward where the laurels grow.

Now or never you must speak
Words to cheer the poor and weak,
Words to comfort those in pain,
Crossed by agony or shame.

Now or never you must lift
High your standard ; life is swift,
And before you seek your rest,
Death may trample o'er your breast.

Now or never you must turn
Skyward, where God's glories burn,
Morning, noon, and starry night,
Seeking for the infinite.

Now or never you must press
To the gates of holiness,
Putting sin and self aside,
And in heaven at last abide.

TO A SCHOOL GIRL.

I OFTEN see you on the street,
  And, with a poet's eyes,
Regard you as a floweret sweet,
  An angel in disguise.

The sunbeams nestle on your face,
  And leave their kisses there,
The wind blows with a careless grace
  Your wealth of auburn hair.

I see you come and see you go,
  With sprightly step and looks,
And ask myself, " Do you suppose
  Her mind is on her books?

" Is she not longing for the time
  To greet her fairy prince,
When love shall speak itself in rhyme,
  And tender thoughts convince? "

A gentle princess, may you rule,
  Dear school girl, young and gay,
When you have said good by to school
  And put your books away.

Consider well the adage old,
  That wise men oft repeat,
The adage that is often told,
  " Whate'er you sow, you reap."

It matters not when down the west
　　Shall ride your Lochinvar,
If love with love is truly blest
　　And goes from star to star.

THE FARMHOUSE 'NEATH THE HILL.

O THE farmhouse 'neath the hill, I can see it standing
　　still,
　As I saw it in my childhood's happy days,
When everything was new and beautiful to view,
　　From morning till the sunset's opal haze.

I can see the orchard trees, and I hear the hum of bees
　　In the hollyhocks and roses near the wall.
And where the brooklet flows, a barefoot urchin goes
　　Again among the cat-o'-nine-tails tall.

Down to the pasture spring I walk and lightly sing,
　　As happy as in merry days gone by,
When I wandered in the wood half lost in solitude,
　　Or climbed the friendly mountain, looming high.

How I love that farmhouse wide, with its trees on either side,
　　Where I played and laughed and wandered when a boy!
I can see the swallows fly down the chimney from the sky,
　　And again I dream a dream of vanished joy.

Wherever I may go, I'll find no place, I know,
　　That will my mind with sweeter fancies fill.
　Fond memory guard the door, and time pass gently o'er
　　That humble old gray farmhouse 'neath the hill.

BEFORE I GO.

BEFORE I go I would that I might sing
 A song to comfort some despairing heart,
Laden with grief, from all the world apart,
  Before I go.

Before I go I would that I might climb
A little higher up the mount of fame,
Braving the storms of envy and disdain,
  Before I go.

Before I go I would that I might look
In trusting eyes and find an answering light,
Knowing that sorrow endeth in delight,
  Before I go.

Before I go I would that I might cheer
Some weary pilgrim on his lonely way,
Shielding from those who startle and betray,
  Before I go.

Before I go I would that I might stay
Some youthful feet from where the spoiler leads,
Warning from evils dark and baleful deeds,
  Before I go.

Before I go I would that I might right
Some grievous wrongs, a deeper feeling share
With all oppressed by suffering and care,
  Before I go.

Before I go I would that I might do
Something to live beyond life's fleeting show.
Give me your hand and say, "I will be true,"
    Before I go.

THE POET'S LIFE.

WHAT is a poet's life at best?
    Men think it only an empty thing
Who are prone to sneer and scoff and jest
    At each skyward fancy taking wing.

What is a poet's life at best?
    The school girl thinks it a life of dreams,
Of beautiful visions fair and blest
    In the land of sunshine and gushing streams.

What is the poet's life at best?
    Some woman thinks it a round of loves,
A feast of pleasure that has no rest,
    A life of roses and turtle doves.

What is a poet's life at best?
    The poet knows it is one of care;
His feet on the thorns of grief have pressed,
    And arm in arm he has walked with prayer.

Although he may die without a thank,
    For sweetest measures receive but slang,
You may call him a fool, a dolt, a crank,
    Yet the world is better because he sang.

THE KING'S DAUGHTERS.

THE pure in heart, the high of soul,
    I hail the royal band
Whose sympathies are with the weak
    And suffering of the land.

Whose faces beam with heavenly rays,
    Sent from the court above,
The gracious offering of our King,
    Whose coronet is love.

I greet them with a brother's prayer,
    Along the narrow way,
And at their shrine I often bow,
    And sweetest tributes lay.

Upon each breast I hail the sign
    Of royalty's decree,
A symbol that will lead them on
    And on to victory.

A passport to the realms of bliss,
    Where living waters flow,
Through the fair city of our God,
    In Eden's golden glow.

The pure in heart, the high of soul,
    For them this meed I bring,
They all are children of the light,
    Dear daughters of the King.

10

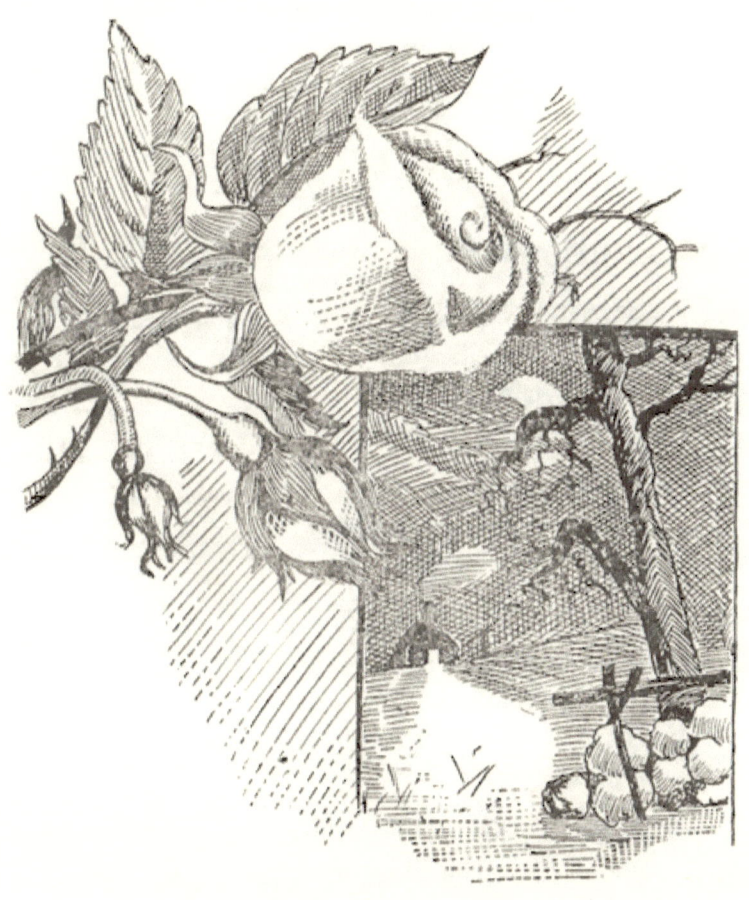

LIFE AND LOVE.

"WHAT is life, can you tell me, pray?"
  I asked a poet I met one day.
The poet smiled and answered me,
"Moonlight and roses and mystery!"

" What is love, can you tell me true ? "
I asked a maiden fair to view.
She blushed and whispered low to me,
" Moonlight and roses and mystery ! "

ON RECEIVING A BLUE RIBBON.

WHILE looking o'er my evening mail,
    Inclosed within a letter,
I found a dainty ribbon blue
    From one,— can I forget her?

I must confess it touched my heart ;
    Remembrances are pleasant,
Whether they come from one as fair
    Or some poor toiling peasant.

It turned my mind to other days,
    I thought of lovers sighing,
And pondered o'er the masters' songs
    Whose music is undying.

I saw the heather covered hills,
    Where roved the ploughman poet.
Had I the genius he possessed
    I know where I 'd bestow it.

I find within this silken band
    The pledge of friendship's token.
O may it ever be the same
    Through life, unchanged, unbroken !

If I could win the love of one
　　As gracious and as tender
As my young friend, with heart and soul
　　I 'd evermore defend her.

THE GIRL I USED TO KNOW.

THE girl I used to know, dear heart, so long ago,
　　Was a charming girl and very, very sweet ;
The color of her eyes was the blue of summer skies,
But my dream of paradise,
　　　　　　　It was fleet.

The girl I used to know, dear heart, I loved her so,
When she died, I grieved for many and many a day,
For her sympathy was wide, and her love seemed like a
　　tide,
Sweeping vanity and pride
　　　　　　　All away.

The girl I used to know, she 's where heavenly breezes
　　blow,
In that happy land beyond the moon and sun,
And where I hope to go, leaving earthly scenes below,
When at last life's fleeting show
　　　　　　　Here is done.

THE OLD TAVERN.

BESIDE the country road it stands,
  A relic of the past,
With rambling roof and gables brown,
  That greet the wintry blast.

Close to its weather-beaten sides,
  The lilac bushes grow,
And near it, in the summer time,
  Old-fashioned roses blow.

I 'm thinking of the days gone by,
  Before the steam cars came,
Of how the stage coach rattled in
  And rattled out again.

I fancy I can hear it now,
  A-coming down the hill,
The tandem team, the cracking whip,
  Plied at the driver's will.

I fancy I can see the boys
  And girls who gathered 'round
The tavern then, to get the news
  And styles from Boston town.

I 'm thinking of the days gone by,
  When, in the vacant hall,
A crowd of lads and lasses gay
  Once held high carnival.

I seem to hear the fiddles play,
    And the gruff prompter's call,
" First couple lead up to the right,"
    And " Swing your pardners all."

Before me, sweeping in a dream,
    The happy dancers glide.
What rosy cheeks !   What smiling lips !
    What haughty love and pride !

What looks of happiness and joy !
    What messages untold !
O memory, to our anxious eyes
    Swing back your gates of gold !

In vain we ask.   The dance is o'er,
    The dancing feet are still.
We listen, but 't is all in vain,
    No stage comes down the hill.

Where once was mirth and social cheer,
    And hearts beat fast and free,
Now all is silent as the grave
    In this old hostelry.

Gone is the merry group that came
    And clustered 'round the door ;
Gone are the pleasant days of old
    From us to come no more.

But still beside the country road,
    Swept by the wintry blast,
The empty tavern, crumbling, stands,
    A relic of the past.

WILLING TO TRY.

" WILL you love, honor, and obey
  This man?" the preacher said
Unto a sweetly gushing bride
 Before the altar led.

She smiled and raised her drooping eyes,
 The bridegroom's face to scan,
Then lowered them again and said,
 "I'll do the best I can."

WE'LL KNOW SOMETIME.

AS through this busy world we go,
 Some honest motives, yours or mine,
May be misjudged, we dream not how,
 But yet I think we'll know sometime.

Why some men win, while others lose,
 Why some should reap where others sow,
We strive in vain to comprehend,
 The secret yet sometime we'll know.

Why some are ever prone to rest,
 While others always seek to climb,
Is still a mystery unsolved,
 But yet I trust we'll know sometime.

Why some are striving after sin,
　　While some are pure as Alpine snow,
We cannot say, but yet I deem
　　The time will come when we shall know

Why some secure love's sweetest flowers,
　　While others weeds and nettles find,
We cannot understand it now,
　　But yet I think we 'll know sometime.

Why some with sorrow bend and grieve,
　　While others happy-hearted go,
With song and jest along the way,
　　The time will come when we shall know.

Why some must drain a bitter cup,
　　While others sip and drink the wine,
With reddened lips and mirthful voice,
　　The answer will be ours sometime.

Why some are ever bound to lead,
　　While others blindly grope below,
The riddle some day we shall guess,
　　The time will come when we shall know.

The time will come when man to man
　　We 'll read life's message true, divine.
Why we have gained, why we have lost,
　　And all the rest, we 'll know sometime.

WALT WHITMAN.

OUR "good grey poet" has from us been borne
  Out of this world into the great unknown,
 Seeking the splendor of some far-off zone,
Whose morning whiteness glimmers and is worn
Upon his brow.   The seal of kingliness
 Is set forever on his patient face,
 Turned starward with the old heroic grace
He knew and felt when life was at its best.
A cannoneer of song, a great artilleryman
 Of thought, who fought life's battles to the close,
 He now has peace, sweet peace and calm repose.
Beyond the tumult that earth's weaklings plan,
 Triumphant o'er the jeers and gibes of foes,
Thou hast the homage our poor words command.

THE MAN WITH THE OVERALLS.

YOU may take for your hero the simpering dude,
  Or the ballroom's petted pride,
Arrayed in all of the latest styles,
 Whose knowledge you say is wide,

With their elegant manners and toney ways,
 Who tip their hats as they pass,
And capture with flattery's lawless wiles
 The heart of many a lass.

With their shining leathers and faultless ties,
　　And the buttonhole bouquets,
We know them ; we've often seen them pass
　　By us on the world's highways.

You may take for your hero the soldier trim,
　　Bright buttons and all of that,
But beside the man with the overalls
　　They often seem poor and flat.

I know him ; his heart is as tender and true
　　As ever was in man's breast,
And his strong right hand is as loyal still
　　As any we ever have pressed.

I know him, for into his eyes I have looked,
　　And found by a mystical sign
Something that many who claim to be men
　　Have lost or can never divine.

He is a hero, I know by his air,
　　Though his clothes may be faded and worn,
As worthy of praise as the hero who dies,
　　And away from the battle is borne.

Though humble his station, the humble may be
　　The great when life's curtain falls,
And over the line we shall some day meet
　　Our friend with the overalls.

HANNAH DUSTIN.

HEROIC woman, thy heroic name we love to speak ;
    It is with honest pride we point to it upon our his-
        tory's page ;
Courageous, daring, not in any age
We read of one more dauntless or discreet,
Beset with dusky foes at Haverhill,
    Who plucked the infant nestling at thy breast,
    And slew it in thy sight. Their murderous quest
At last was ended ; thou redressed the ill
When slumber fell upon the Indian camp,
    After the painful march to Pennacook ;
    Twelve evil lives thou and the brave lad took,
Who had been with thee through the torturing tramp ;
    Upon thy statues many pause and look,
    Thy feature's glow with fame's heroic stamp.

AN EASTER SONG.

THE earth with joy is swelling,
    From winter's bonds set free,
And from each heart is welling
    A song of jubilee.

From hilltop and from mountain
    The joyful tidings ring ;
From every gushing fountain
    We hail our risen King.

The night of gloom has ended,
  Gethsemane is past,
With all its grief attended
  The morning came at last.

O lilies white and tender,
  We find in thee a sign
Of what our hearts may render
  To Him we hold divine.

Bright is the sunlight streaming
  O'er earth and heaven wide.
Rejoice, O sad hearts dreaming!
  Again 't is Eastertide.

BOXED.

"WE'RE in a box," we often say,
    When we are sore perplexed,
And hardly know just what to do,
  Or what to think of next.

We 're in a box, when at the play
  Our seats are near the stage,
Providing we can get the cash
  Such boxes to engage.

We 're in a box when at the court
  We sit as jurymen,—
When we are good for nothing else,
  So says the joker's pen.

We 're in a box when at the last
  We 've given up the fight,
And they have taken us away,
  And put us out of sight.

LOVE AND LIGHTNING.

L OVE and lightning !   Let me see.
      Are they not some alike ?
We never know just when or where
  Or how they both will strike.

The question is, which is the worse ?
  Now answer me who will.
There have been cases, I have heard,
  Where both were known to kill.

And other instances, of course,
  About them we have talked,
Of people that we often meet,
  Who have been slightly shocked.

Before you die, you may get struck
  By the lightning's lurid glare,
But the chances are ten times to one
  'T will be some love affair.

TO A FRIEND.

DO you remember how we walked and stood
    One night beside the river flowing wide,
  That moonlit night, when, wandering side by side,
We paused to dream, as only dreamers could ?
Have you forgotten how the silence yearned
    To find a voice ? how all was calm and still,
    Save for a friendly cricket chirping shrill
His evening notes ? how silently we turned
And wandered back into the city's glare ?
    Our secret thoughts were left behind unsaid,
    As cold and silent as the voiceless dead.
We left them and the river flowing there,
    That autumn night, when all around was spread,
    Nearer than either dreamed, a world of prayer.

NEVER AGAIN.

NEVER again, though the spirit yearneth
    After the things it sought to gain ;
Joy may come, but the past returneth
        Never again.

Never again will love that is tender
    Gladden the hearts where love is slain ;
Waken to life and complete surrender,
        Never again.

TO A YOUNG POET.

Respectfully inscribed to Fred Goldsmith Walker, Salem, Mass.

IN youth's bright morning, vigilant and brave,
  With the great future all before you spread,
O'er flowery meads of song your footsteps tread.
Gifted by God you have the power to save,
To scatter sunbeams o'er each troubled wave
  That beats against some suffering brother's heart,
  To cheer him onward with your tender art,
And point him upward unto Him who gave
His life for others.   From each lowly grave
  The story of the world's frail children read.
  Be ever loyal, both in word and deed,
And not for riches but for goodness crave,
  Seeking the paths where worthy men succeed,
'Till at your feet the tides of fortune lave.

AS WE LOOK BACK.

AS we look back along life's dusty way,
  We find some barren places and some flowers,
Some days of sadness and some sunny hours.
    As we look back.

As we look back some memories give us pain,
  Some bring the tears unbidden to our eyes,
  And some,— Ah ! some shall we not always prize,
    As we look back.

As we look back sweet faces on us smile.
  O happy eyes !   O cheeks with love aglow !
  O little hands, your vanished thrill we know,
      As we look back !

As we look back the bitterness and gall,
  The things that tried us on our lonely way,
  Now haunt us less but dimmer grow each day,
      As we look back.

As we look back the milestones, one by one,
  Gleam gray and white beside the old and new.
  We pause, for soon may come the last review,
      As we look back.

As we look back the battlefields of doubt
  Are strewn with skeletons of passions slain.
  What first seemed loss at last we found was gain.
      As we look back.

As we look back how tenderly we dwell
  O'er the old places vanished from our sight ! ·
  What fruitful themes that move the pen to write,
      As we look back.

As we look back we know that God was true,
  That He will lead us down life's dusty track.
  Still for his favors let us humbly sue,
      As we look back.